GAWAIN

AND

LADY GREEN

By the same author:
Merlin's Harp

GAWAIN
AND
LADY
GREEN

Anne Eliot Crompton

DONALD I. FINE BOOKS
New York

Donald I. Fine Books
Published by the Penguin Group
Penguin Books USA Inc., 375 Hudson Street,
New York, New York 10014, U.S.A.
Penguin Books Ltd, 27 Wrights Lane,
London W8 5TZ, England
Penguin Books Australia Ltd, Ringwood,
Victoria, Australia
Penguin Books Canada Ltd, 10 Alcorn Avenue,
Toronto, Ontario, Canada M4V 3B2
Penguin Books (N.Z.) Ltd, 182–190 Wairau Road,
Auckland 10, New Zealand

Penguin Books Ltd, Registered Offices:
Harmondsworth, Middlesex, England

First published by Donald I. Fine Books,
an imprint of Penguin Books USA Inc.

First Printing, April, 1997

10 9 8 7 6 5 4 3 2 1

LIBRARY OF CONGRESS CATALOGING-IN-PUBLICATION DATA
Crompton, Anne Eliot.
Gawain and Lady Green / Anne Eliot Crompton.
p.   cm.
ISBN 1-55611-507-5
1. Gawain (Legendary character)— I. Title.
PS3553.R539G38   1997
813′.54—dc20   96-44145
CIP

Printed in the United States of America
Set in 11/14 New Aster

Alone in Time your Poem stands,
A Great Hall ruling rugged lands;
Your words its walls, its hearth your heart.
Along your wall I add a room apart;
A garden door ajar; green, leafy light,
A turning trail that travels out of sight.

THE
GREEN
CROWN

A GREAT WHITE HORSE stood hidden, almost invisible, on the edge of the oak grove. Its dark young rider looked across a stream to the Fair-Field. In the midst a maypole reared to the spring sky, all a-flutter with strung leaves and flowers.

So! The young man thought, or tried to think. Hunger and fatigue numbed his mind. *So this must be May Day. Spring.*

The endless winter he had ridden through—at first provisioned, and now starving; at first in company, and now alone—the terrible winter was over.

A crowd of merry savages milled about the maypole: uncouth men armed only with staves, bright-gowned women with flowers in their braids. Yapping children and dogs sped from one small fire to the next, from one loaded table to the next.

Loaded tables.

The young knight's starved stomach cried, *God's blessed eyes! Meat on the spit!* Heart leaped high, with all the proud confidence that was his heritage. Not for a moment did he hesitate.

Straightway he clapped heels to horse. Through the shallow, stony stream they splashed, up the bank, onto the Fair-Field. He steered straight for the nearest table.

According to God's Natural Law this bumpkin crowd should give way promptly before a mounted knight. He could wolf down half a pig haunch before they rounded up their chief, druid or headman, to deal with him. And by then he would have his wits and manners back in order. But at this moment the smell of roasting meat overwhelmed all protocol, all courtesy. It was not as though he dealt with equals here.

But this crowd gave him no way.

Warrior, his white charger, pushed narrowly between two arguing women. A startled fellow wheeled around and grabbed for his rein.

"Make way!" The hungry young knight shouted warning. "Ho, hey, give way there!" The rasp of his own voice startled him. He had not spoken in many a day. "What are you folk? Stand back!—God's teeth!"

The crowd closed in. He clapped hand to sword hilt.

Too late.

Hands seized Warrior's bridle. Hands grabbed arm, foot, scabbard, and yanked. He was on the ground, men piled heavy on top. Boots stamped before his eyes. Above, hunters halloed.

Mary shield me!

Hooves tramped around his head as the crowd pushed and pulled at Warrior. He heard the sword screech out of his scabbard. Ripped off, his helmet rolled among feet.

The weight of men lifted off him. Now the sword would come down. *That I should die by the hands of savages!*

Hands seized him and hauled him to his feet. *Maybe not yet?*

Strong-twined rope pulled his arms tight. *What do they want?*

Warrior's white rump disappeared into the mob.

Move. Walk. Not so fast, the way I'm trussed! . . . This way. The maypole.

Horns shouted. A screaming wind blew away hearing; bagpipes, too close. Now the crowd opened a path to the maypole; and all along the path merry eyes beamed and orange-green teeth gleamed through beards. Near fluttered wind-waved strung flowers and leaves. High rose the may-pole into spring-morning sky. *Now we're here, what—*

Horns and pipes fell abruptly silent. The jabbering mob fell silent.

At the maypole's foot they let him go. They stood back and left him bruised, swaying in his bonds, dizzy with hunger, confused past surprise.

Three faces confronted him. A white-haired druid held with both hands a crown of flowers high over the head of a stiff-faced, pale young man. A girl held the man's hand, a sturdy peasant girl, clad all in green, her rich red hair already flower-crowned. The three stared, astonished, at the dark young man reeling in his bonds. Slowly, the girl smiled.

Her smile lit her plain face, and the fluttering leaf-strings above, and the spring-green air all about. Her green gown flowed to her ankles, held at the hips by a green lace girdle. Gown and girdle, hands, arms, and neck were looped or studded with green-gold gems.

She smiled. She let go of the stiff-faced fellow's hand. The white-bearded druid nodded one deep, slow nod.

Two women burst from the crowd. Joyfully, they grabbed the stiff-faced fellow by the arms and pulled him away backward. The crowd swallowed him up.

The druid stepped up to the captive. Keen old blue eyes met mystified grey young eyes. Trembling, upraised hands came down. Like an enemy's ax, the crown of flowers descended upon the captive's head.

Air roared again as drums rumbled and pipes wailed. Knives sliced the knight's bonds.

The red-haired girl seized his hand and pulled him into a jigging dance. Hungered and aching, he could hardly keep up. He waddled after her like a leashed dancing bear.

Drums and pipes merged rhythms. The girl leaped, the knight lumbered. Dancers joined them around the maypole. The blowing maypole ribbons tightened as they were caught in dancers' hands, shortened as they were twined together. Out in the field the whole crowd danced. The Fair-Field danced. Earth danced.

The knight thought, *If I can but go along* . . .

As a young child he had danced around maypoles. He began to master the step. The girl grinned over her shoulder and squeezed his hand harder. Jigging became easier than stumbling. Heart took on drum-rhythm. Pipes screeched in the blood. The girl's loose red hair fanned his face. Something jogged down over his eyes so that he danced blind; the flower crown. A friendly hand reached from behind and straightened it. But it inched down again and flopped about his neck.

He had danced in place for a while before the girl stopped him, smiling, hands on his shoulders. Music and dance had paused. The maypole stood wrapped, bright against mild sky. A band of wild, masked men all in green now cavorted around it, waving hawthorn branches and tumbling. The crowd applauded.

Hazy, the captive found himself leaning against a table. A hand held a mug of ale under his nose. He seized it and drained the contents.

Then he sneezed foam and grabbed at the table for support. A close-by voice asked a question. Though soft, the voice was uncouth, northernly accented, the words hard to understand. "What?" With the back of his hands he rubbed away foam and sweat.

The flower-crowned girl stood close.

Now he saw her clear; under all the green finery and frip-frap, a vigorous, full body; work-roughened, square hands; hard grey eyes, wide now with wonder—she might never have seen his like before.

And he had never seen her like before quite like this, face to face and equal. Softly, now; he had come into a foreign world here, almost as if he had entered Fairyland. In Fairyland there was no telling what or who it was that you saw. A toad could be a prince, a wild tribal girl could be . . .

Very courteously he asked her, "Did you speak to me, Lady Green?"

Laughter flashed across her peasant face. She spoke again. Listening attentively, he barely understood her.

"I asked you, What is your name?"

"My name is Gawain, Lady. I am Sir Gawain of the Round Table."

"*Sir* Gawain. Aha. Are you a knight, Sir Gawain of the Round Table?"

"Surely you know—" He checked himself. "Yes, Lady Green, I am a King's Companion." And nephew—but no need to say that.

A face butted in between them. For a dazed moment, Gawain thought it the face of an ancient white goat. In a clearer accent than the girl's it said, "I have heard of you, Sir Gawain, King's Companion." It was the old druid, the flower-crowner. "What do you here, with us?"

"I . . ." How best to put this? Ale fought with exhaustion on Gawain's tongue. "My king sent me here to . . . see the north country."

"Hah! To spy. Did you come here alone?"

"No, Father." Very polite. "Three of us came, with squires and horses and packhorses bearing gifts. We came as emissaries."

"Hah. Gladly would we see these emissaries and these gifts. Where are they?"

"Father, we met brigands."

"Naturally. But you were armed."

"Then we met Saxons. We were sadly outnumbered. Then there came wolves."

"Four-legged ones." The old man grinned. "And you alone are left?"

"I, and my horse, which should be somewhere near." The great, valuable charger would prove his worth to these savages.

The druid would have answered, but the girl spoke up boldly, startling Gawain. Little courtesy or caution here! He understood her to say, "I never saw a knight before." She studied him carefully, sweat-dark hair to travel-ragged boots. "But I will know you well tonight." Her quick smile flashed.

Uncomprehending, Gawain stared.

The old druid explained. "You are crowned May King, Sir Gawain. You lie tonight with the May Queen. Did you not know?"

Gawain found his tongue. "I . . . Yes. I have heard of such." But not for a while.

"Show him food," Druid told Girl. "He's in no shape now, but with meat in his belly . . ."

Once more Gawain found himself led by the hand. The Green Men still leaped and capered, the crowd still applauded; but Gawain saw nothing, was aware of nothing but roast meat and bread that smoked on the table where the May Queen led him.

Pig meat! Breads! Ale! Eating and talking, the crowd came around them. When Gawain took notice again, he saw only joyful cordiality everywhere. Men who had seized and bound him now clapped his back, all friendly. Women who had halloed over him as over a stuck pig now plied him with food. Children stared up at his flower necklace, awed, and nearly polite. Good fellowship surrounded him like springtime. Astonished dread, watchful loneliness, melted like snow. With every bite, every handclasp, more of the brave young Sir Gawain of yore strengthened and took shape in the sunlight. Spine straightened; step light-ened; he knew again the familiar, dark sound of his own friendly voice.

Wandering, mug in hand, he came upon a hunk of shoulder-meat spitted over a small fire. At his feet lay shreds and scraps of bloody white horsehide. Nearby—

God's teeth! That's my saddle! The King's stamped straps still on it! And there's my pack . . . empty . . .

And this meat must be my Warrior.

His stomach turned inside out. He retched, caught himself, clapped hand to sword.

No sword. Empty scabbard.

Right. They got the sword away, first thing.

The very recent memory swam vaguely in his mind.

No more of that ale. Ech! He flung the mug aside.

Sad and sickened, he stared down at the remains. "Who is Sir Gawain, afoot and swordless? Who am I now?"

He must have murmured aloud. A voice at his ear answered, uncouth but loving. "You are our May King, Gawain. My May King. You will understand that tonight, to your joy and my own." Warm and solid, she leaned into his shoulder. Her hair mantled his arm. The scent of her fading flower crown overwhelmed him.

Brave young Sir Gawain of yore rose to her challenge. He turned and embraced her, drew her in, caressed and kissed her, there in the crowd's midst under spring sunlight. And forgot all else.

"WELL, FOR SURE AND certain," said Old Lady Granny, "you knew it weren't just for the one night!"

Solid she sat on her hut doorsill, spinning. Fingers gnarled with age still twirled the thread swiftly down from the distaff in her hand to the bobbin swinging at her feet. When she tossed her thick grey braid back over her shoulder the gesture was almost seductive, almost worthy of her granddaughter, Lady Green. She smiled through a map of close wrinkles at Gawain, where he sat on a stool brought out from the hut. Hens clucked and scratched around his feet. An old brindled dog sunned beside him.

" 'Course you have to go on, all summer, till Summerend itself. That's how the grain grows, you know—with your lovin'. Your love flows into the grain, and it grows. Don't you know nothin', Fellow?"

Gawain forgot to repress a small shudder at her easy "Fellow." She chuckled and glimmered at him, teasing.

He had lost track of time. He knew he had been here in this tribal village of Holy Oak for many days, more than half a moon. After May Day they had taken away his own clothes and given him theirs—rough wool tunic and cloak, hide boots that tied to the knee. His black beard had thickened to where he could chew long strands of it. He cleaned his teeth halfheartedly with alder twigs. He thought that Lancelot, or even his own brothers, seeing him, would take him for a village knave. Except for his stance. Except for his knightly walk.

He straightened his shoulders and smiled back at the old dame.

She continued. "That's why you love in the fields, clear nights. So the love ain't got far to go. 'Course you have to go on. Why, don't you know nothin', Son? Where do you come from, anyhow?"

"From the south, Lady. From King Arthur's Dun."

"And they don't do nothin' down there? How's their barley grow, then?"

He thought on it. "Shrovetide, priests bless the fields. The villagers go through the fields in procession, singing and praying."

"Ech, aye, that must help it grow. But is that all?"

"All that I know of. Well, no. There's prayers for sun when it's needed, and even for rain."

Sniff. "Seldom knew rain to be needed! Prayer's good, and singin' and all. But it don't sound like enough."

Gawain shrugged politely. "They usually reap a good crop."

"They? Who's 'they'? Aren't you in on this yourself?"

How ignorant could even a northern savage be? "I . . . no, Lady Granny. I am a knight."

"So what do you do, Knight?"

"I fight for my King."

"All the time?"

"I hunt with my King. I feast at his Round Table. I hold myself ready to serve him."

"And that's all you do?"

"Lady, I am a skilled, strong fighter."

"Aye, I can see that." Twirl, twirl went the busy thread.

Unbidden, the child piped up. "He's famous, Granny. There's songs about him. Ma told me." Her voice grated unchildishly.

"Ynis," the old lady snapped, "mind your thread."

Lady Green's little girl sat on the chopping block beside the hut door. Her small, tapered fingers twirled the thread awkwardly. Even Gawain's untrained eye observed knots and uneven, fraying sections in it.

Unused to children, Gawain put her age at six, maybe seven years. He marveled that young, fresh Lady Green was old enough to have birthed this child. Ynis was dark as her mother was bright, thin as her mother was buxom. Her round child's face—even missing two front teeth—gave promise of beauty to surpass her mother's. Gawain had noticed before this her awkwardness, her uneasiness with common tasks and skills.

11

Now she looked up from the troublesome thread and feasted her eyes on the barley field below the village.

"Feasted her eyes," Gawain mused, was the right phrase. Her strange, unchildish gaze wondered and widened. The half-size distaff dropped unheeded in her grey wool lap.

"Look, Granny," she said dreamily. "She's out there now."

Lady Granny swung around abruptly. She shaded her eyes and followed the child's gaze. "Aye," she breathed. "So She is." And her bobbin hung idle.

Curious, Gawain turned on his stool to look out over the land.

The village of unkempt thatched huts squatted on a plateau looking three ways. Northward stretched pastureland, dotted with groves and herds. Northeast lay the Fair-Field, the place of concourse for this and two other villages. East along the stream straggled the all-important crops: fields and fenced patches of grains, peas, and beans, crisscrossed with trails. Now, between the trails, a soft green spread across brown, tilled earth as the seeds sprouted.

(South, behind the village, rose a great, dark oak grove where folk did not go. Lady Green kept a bower there, a wee hut where she lay with Gawain on rainy nights. From a low wing of this grove Gawain had burst so rashly upon the busy Fair-Field, ages ago. Gazing now, he thought he saw again the crowded field, the bright maypole, and himself on his white Warrior, trotting confidently into the midst, making for the nearest table. He shook his head, growled at himself, and dismissed the fancy.)

Today the Fair-Field stretched empty but for a near band of boys hunting rabbits and a far flock of strayed sheep.

Eastward the crops broke earth, reaching their fresh,

sweet greenness to the sun. Not even Gawain, born noble
and raised for knighthood, could look upon this rising life
and promise entirely unmoved. A primal, unthought joy
drew heart up out of body for a moment, and in that moment he prayed, *God-thank.*

Small Ynis piped, "She's getting bigger. Look, Granny.
She was like a person, a . . . a mother. Standing in the
peas. Now She's like a tree. Watch Her spread out!"

"Aye," Lady Granny said calmly, "She can spread like
mist, or cloud. She can cover the world. Or She can dance
on your little finger."

What She? Straining his eyes, Gawain saw only sunshine and spring-greening crops. An invisible, suspicious
finger touched his mind. He shivered.

"There, She's fading . . . like a rainbow." Disappointment lowered the child's voice.

"She don't really fade," Granny explained. " 'Tis but
our sight fades. She's still there."

Granny jiggled her bobbin back into action. Ynis
looked to Gawain. (Anywhere but to her tangled thread!)
She remarked, "His cloud's a mighty funny color."

Granny's shrewd old eyes crinkled at Gawain. "Mind
your manners, Ynis. And your thread."

To Gawain she said lightly, "Don't you be feared of us,
Son."

Gawain, feared? Feared of these two crazies? He stiffened angrily.

Ynis said, "See? Now his cloud's turned all red."

"We're just two crazies," Granny confirmed his
thought. "Just touched, that's all we are. Dreamin' together."

That was plain to see. These two dreamed in daylight?
Let them. It was their village, Gawain sat on their stool,
and would soon drink their mead. He could hear Lady
Green now moving about inside the hut, preparing it.

13

Gawain drew a calming breath. He had no cause for anger. Or fear.

"Now his cloud's brighter," Ynis observed.

Granny asked her sweetly, "You want a clout on the ear?"

Ynis fell silent.

If only the whole village did not seem touched! It was fine to be looked on as some sort of angel or pagan God, to be revered and bowed to and politely pushed to the head of every line. That was but a knight's due among poor, ignorant savages. But, ech! Uneasily, Gawain knew they did not revere him as knight, as noble, or as King's Companion. They did not honor his warrior's fame, as would be only right.

Something here was amiss, mysterious. The whole village seemed somehow . . . off.

Ech. He would have to humor them. Here he sat, unarmed in their midst. And they did him no harm. To the contrary! Southward, King Arthur in his Dun reigned no more comfortably than Sir Gawain, May King, reigned here in Holy Oak.

And yet, if only he had a horse . . .

Leather hinges creaked. His Lady Green stooped through the hut doorway, a brimming mug cradled in her hands. She smiled at him, and all the day's bright sunshine brightened still more.

Dressed in a sober grey workaday gown, she yet wore green about her: a leaf bracelet, one green-stone ring, one green-stemmed wind flower caught in her swinging red braid. (At night she always came to Gawain gowned and girdled in green.)

She rested a hand on Granny's shoulder, stepped down from doorsill to ground, and straightened. Dignified as Queen Gwenevere herself, she walked toward Gawain, smiling, holding out the mug of brimming mead. Something in her calm, free walk stirred a memory. Somewhen, someone Gawain had loved had walked like that. But who? But when?

Come, sir! (said his talkative Inner Mind). *You are but twenty-six, you cannot have forgotten that much yet!*

But it would not come to him.

Tell you one thing (Inner Mind spoke again), *you've never lain with a woman like this one before!*

He reached out for the mug, drawing nearer.

Experience there, for all she's so young. She's taught you much already.

So, what are you grumbling about? Accept this summer as an adventure! An enterprise old Merlin can sing about. "Gawain, May King!" That's the song he'll sing one day. The whole kingdom will sing it. For now, enjoy!

Gawain looked up into Lady Green's shining, smiling eyes. He took the mug she offered and gulped its contents to the dregs.

NIGHT RAIN-MUSIC IS MY favorite sound.

Night rain sings softly of summer, of growing crops, of sleep—and so, of love.

I lie here against my May King, head on his arm. Deeply he breathes beside me, catching back well-spent breath. His heart flutters under my hand like a caught bird.

My bower bends low above us. I look up into its arched branches by dim lamplight. Up there, thick thatch I gathered and bound, dried, and laid catches rain and sends it sliding away all richly wet.

Above in the rain-sweet dark, ancient oaks guard the

bower. Heavy in my happy body, I listen to night rain whisper joy in their leaves.

An owl calls, sudden and near. From the eastern edge of the grove, another answers.

My May King starts. He turns to me, draws me closer. The lamp sputtering beside our pallet shows me his smile, his slowly opening eyes.

He is one strange fellow, this Sir Gawain from the south!

I have known men. But never a man so rigid-proud in body and mind.

Despite his pride, he knows nothing. When he first came, he could not even understand speech easily.

Like a young child—like my daughter, Ynis—he most often speaks to ask a question. Ynis asks, "Why do we have to card wool?" Gawain asks, "Why do folk stay away from the oak grove?" No one past toddling should need to ask such questions!

Angry once, in his quick, easy anger, he told me I would need to ask questions in his world! "You think me child-ignorant?" He spluttered. "You go south to Arthur's Dun, lady, we'll see who's the child there!"

A good thing it is I will never have to try that out.

But I myself do not know quite everything. There are things I have been wondering about him.

Now as his eyes open wide grey in lamplight, his lips open to question. I lay a finger across them, and he stills.

"My turn to question, May King. I want to know a thing, and it is this: How came you here to this place, to Holy Oak village, out of the south?" I lift my finger away to let him answer.

"I came a-horse, Lady Green."

I love that name! Lady Green can only be the mirror of the Green Goddess! I will be Lady Green only and always for him. And because he gave me this sweet, so-dignified name a loving bard might have invented, I like his name too. I speak it now with teasing tenderness. "Gawain, I know full well that you came a-horse!"

"And I have asked the headman, and Merry the druid—"

"The student druid. It takes years to turn druid."

"I have asked them both to replace my butchered charger; for they two seem more the leaders here than any others. I know you have horses at pasture."

"Not chargers, Gawain. Ponies."

"Aye, little northern ponies no winter lack can kill. I've seen your herds out there. Better a pony than afoot!"

"But I asked you, how did you come here. You said you were spying the land."

"Mapping. Learning. Not spying."

"But the north country is huge, Gawain. How did you come out right there, on that edge of the grove by the Fair-Field? When you had the wide north and west to roam."

"Ech. As to that, I followed a doe here."

"Ah?"

"A white fallow doe. I saw her from afar, white against dark trees. The first trees I had seen all day."

"White. You're sure she was white."

"Milk-white. Snow-white. And I was a-hungered, Lady Green!"

I chuckle. "Well I remember you hungry!"

"So I clapped spur after her. And she ran into this grove and disappeared. And there was the Fair-Field."

"I see . . ." I see more and farther than Gawain will ever guess.

"And had I known you wanted a May King to help the crops grow, I would have turned back away, unseen!"

"You are ungallant, May King!" He taught me this peevish, lilting phrase that southern ladies use in his King's Dun.

17

"No." His arm comes around me heavy as iron, warm as June. "It is well enough. I am content. We two go well together."

In truth!

"But you're wearing me out, I'll admit that."

"Nothing a night's rest won't cure."

"Maybe. But tell me, how can a man rest beside you, Lady Green?"

"Now that's gallant."

"But answer me this." Ech, here comes a question! "A thing I've wondered. If I'm the May King, I help the crops grow, and everyone bows to the ground to me . . ." An exaggeration ". . . could I lie with any woman but you, May Queen? Supposing you were ugly and angry as a spider? Could I lie elsewhere?"

Strange, how an icicle pricks my heart!

I lie silent. Night rain sings in oak leaves and thatch. Gawain's arm weighs down my waist.

"Lady Green?"

At last I answer. "Yes. You could. You can do anything you want."

"Anything at all."

"Almost. No one will refuse you anything. Certainly not something as harmless as that."

"The headman and Student Merry refuse me a horse!"

"They want to keep you here with us. We all do."

"For your God-blasted crops!" Quick anger rises in his voice.

"For our Goddess-blessed crops." Wipe out the blasphemy She may have heard.

Quick, now. Turn his quick anger away.

Light-voiced, I tease. "You can lie with anyone you want, Gawain, but I warn you. Better not!"

His arm tightens on my waist as he chuckles. "Now

you sound like a woman of my own country. A wedded wife."

I am somewhat curious about the women Gawain has known. "You say that gravely, Gawain. In your country, what does a wedded wife do?"

"She keeps her husband strictly to herself. Or she tries to."

"We have rules about that."

"So do we. But only the wife must truly obey them."

"What?" With both hands I lift Gawain's arm off me. Truly curious now, I rise on an elbow and look down on him. "Only the wife must be faithful? What sort of rule is that?"

"A practical one." He smiles up at me. "The husband is the stronger. Shall we two try that out now?"

"Gawain, answer me! Why should the husband not be as faithful as the wife?"

"Well." His fingers tease my breast that leans over him. I draw back, sit up. Wrap arms about knees. He sighs.

"In the south, Lady Green, the husband is master in all ways. The wife's property belongs to him. The wife belongs to him. She keeps his house, comforts his body, bears his sons."

"And what does he do for her?"

"He guards and maintains her, and the house, and the sons."

"And the daughters?"

"He marries them off to useful friends and allies."

I am not like Gawain, easily angered. But I feel my breath come a little fast and anxious. "And have these women of yours no power at all?"

"They wear no swords." Gawain smiles up at me. Smile and fingers beckon. "Come, Lady Green. Lie down again by me."

I stay where I am, wrapped in cool wrath. "Let me

warn you, May King. Spirit is stronger than a hundred swords."

Gawain pulls a doubtful, merry face.

Thought stabs, knife-sharp. "And you, Gawain. Are you wed? Do you have a faithful wife back in your own country?"

Instant answer. "No, Lady Green."

"Hah." Relief. "Then you owe your—what is that word?—fealty, only to me."

Instant, serious answer. "No, Lady Green."

"What! What? You said—"

Gravely. "I owe my fealty to my King."

"Hah." His king. A different kind of fealty altogether. Very well. I let tension out in a slow sigh and lie down against him. "Your king . . . Arthur. I have heard Druid Merlin sing of him."

Gawain stiffens. He goes all still as if a spirit touched him. Then he rises in his turn and leans above me.

"Merlin? Mage Merlin? Merlin has come here, to this God-forgotten place?"

"He comes now and then. Often at Midsummer. When the sky smiles, and the Green Men dance. Then he comes and sings to us of far kings and gods and heroes. You know him, Gawain?"

"God's teeth! Old Merlin, here!" His face shines brighter than the lamp. Even in dim light I see his aura now, what Ynis calls his "cloud." It flames out from him, green with sudden hope.

"This Midsummer when he comes, I will escort him back south!"

No!

I act a delicate yawn. "Not so fast, May King." Not near so fast.

"You will have to find me a horse!"

"Later. When your task is done."

"You expect me to wait here till Summerend itself?"

"Why, yes, Gawain. Till the grain is scythed. Come, now." I bring his hand back to my breast. "If you are so eager to leave me, let us urge the crops a little higher tonight."

Near and far, three owls hoot.

Later Gawain dozes, head on my shoulder, arm across my hips. Steady feet slog stealthily past in steady rain. Gawain murmurs, "Someone besides us braves this mysterious grove tonight."

I stroke his coarse black hair. "Only the watchman, love."

He raises his head. In the lamp's last light I see his eyes—open, clear, quite conscious. "They guard us, Lady Green. Those watchmen. Why do they guard us all night?"

"May King, you are precious to all of us. Nothing must happen to you. Nothing at all." I smile up into his too conscious eyes. "Let me up. I'll get your drink."

Obedient, he drinks, lies back and sleeps. I watch him almost tenderly.

He is one beautiful fellow, this Sir Gawain from the south! Hard, lean, lusty as a buck goat, though not skilled in love. I like the thought that I may be one of his first lovers. I like to teach.

Such Goddess-blessed vigor should be preserved in this green world. The life should outlive the man.

When he sleeps, his aura rises gently away. Daytimes, it clings close to his body, a narrow orange-brown cloud. But at night, I sometimes see it, dim in lamplight, rise white, and broaden, and drift away south.

Besides his useful, lovely body, he has a soul.

Unwilling, unwise, I feel for him.

God's bones! gawain's softened hands rejoiced to handle steel again! Though a scythe was at best an unfamiliar tool. Student Druid Merry had shown him how to grasp it: "Here and here, May King. Not like a sword."

Merry smiled with beardless lips and warm brown eyes. Small and agile, crowned with gold-brown curls, he struck Gawain as slightly Fey. Strange that one like this should appear to lead men! Yet, maybe not so strange. Close to the fellow, Gawain felt leashed power stir under bouncing curls and easy smile.

Perhaps as a small child Gawain might have handled a scythe. The bend-and-swing motion, which he copied from the men beside him, came easily enough. It did not last as well. Sweat sprang and dripped from brow, stripped chest and shoulders. Bent back and bowed legs screamed.

Stubbornly he thought, *The grass is my enemy. The battle rages.* And he charged ahead of the slowly advancing line.

"Hoo!" His neighbors called. "You, May King! Leave grass enough for us!" Whistles and laughter rippled along the line.

Gawain paused to let them catch up. How good it felt to straighten his spine! With bare forearms he swiped sweat from his eyes and saw clearly, for a moment, the field of wild-weed grass sway ahead. Larks sprang up from hidden nests. At Gawain's feet a serpent writhed desperately away.

God's blood! The company of men, the rough smell and sound of men, felt good! Like food after hunger, like rest after love.

They were all here, all the men he saw about the village, with their sons. Even the old headman scythed, and Student Merry, though these two were the closest to nobility that Gawain found here.

He had met the men and boys at the latrine pits, all joking and flexing, all eager to work. Laughing and friendly, they had invited him along. Merry had whipped the straw hat off his own head and set it on Gawain's. "Against the sun, May King. Heat will be our enemy today."

Bored to exhaustion with luxury, Gawain had come.

He had time now to gasp, swipe sweat once again, and judge the distance to the shade trees where they had left their lunch. A long, long way.

The line came up to him. Bending to scythe again, he gritted his teeth. The man on his left grinned across. "That speed, May King, you'll never make lunch!"

From the right, "Slow and steady—"

From farther along, "Right and ready—"

"Win my wager!"

So, the bumpkins were wagering on him! Like men-at-arms watching a cockfight, or a joust.

Except that they were all jousting too.

Gawain grinned at his neighbors and attacked the grass. Slowly.

At long, long last he scythed his way into tree shade. His heart pounded, his breath rasped, as though he had just come off a battle. Gratefully he downed scythe and shade hat, straightened and stretched along with his neighbors.

One clapped his shoulder. "Not bad," he guffawed, blowing breath like the downwind of slaughter in Gawain's face. "If you're picky about your hay." To the others he yelled, "Only the best for the May King!"

Puzzled, Gawain turned to look at his back-trail.

The field lay fairly cut, except for here and there stalks and clumps boys had missed; and except for a long zigzag path of misses where Gawain himself had staggered and swung.

Laughter, back-pounding, bet-collecting. Lunch.

Cheerfully, young Merry shared his loaf, cheese, and ale with Gawain. They sat backed against a beech trunk in the deepest shade. The rest lay about or sat on their heels, munching and gulping in suddenly tired silence. As the sun crossed the tree line men stretched out on backs and sides and snored. A few boys trotted about the near, uncut field in a halfhearted game.

A handful of top men came into the beech shade with Merry and Gawain. Gawain knew their rank not by dress or title but only by their gaze and bearing.

One said to him, "No offense, May King. But you scythe as though never before. Like my boy over there. How can that be?"

Gawain nursed the last of Merry's ale. "I am a warrior, a knight, born and raised. Where I come from, knights do not scythe."

The men murmured. Another asked, "Where you come from, are there wars every day? That much fighting to do?"

"In truth, not now. The wars ended when Arthur became High King."

"Aha! When he pulled sword from stone, as bards sing."

"No, that was but the beginning. Not all men accepted his kingship. We had to ram it down their throats," Gawain said with relish.

Murmurs. Stirrings.

"So what do you southern knights do now, instead of work?"

"Keep in shape."

Mumbled chuckles.

"We stand war-ready at every moment. Some underking might challenge Arthur again any day. We guard his

Dun, hunt with him, ride the kingdom with him. Joust to keep in practice."

"Joust? What's this joust?"

"Fight mock battles. Singly, or as small armies."

"Ho! That's the life, Brothers!"

"More fun than farming."

"What say, May King? You want to show us a trick now?"

Smiling carefully, Gawain shook his head. "No horses." (Softly, now. This might just be a way to get on a horse!)

"Horses! You joust a-horse?"

"Hey-hoo! I'd like to see a joust!"

"I'd like to joust a joust."

"May King, you must show us how!"

"Very well." Very calm. But hope leaped like a lark in Gawain's breast. Once a-horse, well out from the village, he might break away free. With luck. With God and Mary's help.

Doon, a knave barely past boyhood, called out, "Ha, May King! Bards sing of King Arthur's Round Table."

Proudly, "I am of the Round Table myself."

"Are you, now? Well, I say, let us be the Square Table!" Doon flashed a grin from startled face to eager face. "The May King here can show us how. And we'll give a show at Summerend, one of these here jousts. Eh, May King?"

"Hmmm." Thoughtfully, Gawain smiled. "Very well." Very well in truth!

"That'll be a show to rival the Green Men!"

"Maybe the Square Table can put on a show every feast time forever!"

Gawain said thoughtfully, "You must show me your methods." They would be useful for Arthur to know.

The bumpkins broke off their happy banter to stare at him. "Methods?"

"Ways of fighting. Weapons."

"Oh. As to those . . ." With gestures they showed him, there and then. He found little difference between their sparring and that of the boys out in the sun.

Surprise loosened his jaw. "You have never been fight-trained?"

"There's refinements." A few more refined warriors showed him those.

"God's bones! Where I come from . . ." But why was he surprised? In truth, they were but a gang of mowers and ploughmen. Dirt-movers. Had he for a moment forgotten that?

He glanced from sun-speckled face to face. In this friendly morning he had learned these faces. Now he saw lines of merriment, of kindness, of temper; bleary eyes, bright eyes, sober and dull; pock marks, lost teeth, scars, bumps.

Inner Mind remarked, *You're seeing men here like yourself. Like your Round Table brothers. Not just bumpkins anymore.*

That's as well. Now I won't underestimate them.

But forget not, Sir—they are indeed only ploughmen.

One reminded him, "You've been trained to fight and nothing else, May King."

Chuckles rippled through the shade. "Never held a scythe before!"

Student Druid Merry said, "Tell us somewhat about your life."

Questions pattered then like rain in leaves.

Gawain told them of his education in Arthur's Dun, how he had grown from page to squire to knight aspirant.

Children, waking in the shade, rubbed their eyes and

listened. Boys who had been wandering the field came back into the shade and listened.

Gawain told them how he had knelt in Arthur's chapel all night, sword upright in his hands, eyes on the altar. Telling, he relived that last night of simple youth. Candles flickered again in his sleepy eyes. The glowing altar lamp spoke again of Christ's True Presence. The wooden Mary, Queen of Heaven, smiled as he nodded, startling him awake.

Consciously, soberly, he gathered up his thoughtless youth and freedom and gave them into her keeping.

"The next day Arthur knighted me." Again the sword laid its man-sized burden of Honor, Fealty, and Chivalry on his young shoulder, then lifted away. Once more in a high and holy moment Gawain became Man and Knight. Astonished, he found his sight tear-dimmed.

Impressed, his audience sighed. Then Merry said, "One matter more. You've mentioned no mother, no father."

"I came young to Arthur's Dun." He had ridden there on a wee island pony. "Truth, I barely remember my parents."

"They had names?"

Gawain hesitated. His position here in Holy Oak was risky enough. Knowing his connections, even these bumpkins might think to use him as a hostage.

But he could not lie. He had never lied since Arthur's sword lay on his shoulder.

"Lot," he admitted. "King of the Orkneys. And Morgause, his wife."

Whistles and growls.

Aroused, Merry leaned forward. "This Morgause," he asked seriously. "Is she not a famous witch?"

God's bones! Here it rose again to haunt him, this

ghost of his past. Even here, they had heard of his mother. "Aye, that she is." He had to admit it.

Merry looked him up and down with new eyes. "We have heard of her. Druid Merlin sings of her."

Gawain shrugged. Strange that Lot, King of the Orkneys, seemed lost in his wife's sinister shadow. But as long as they did not know—

"Another matter with Morgause," Merry pursued. "Is she not a sister of your king?"

"Aye. That she is."

"King Arthur is your uncle."

"Aye."

"Heh! By the Grove Gods!" Merry leaned back against the beech and closed his eyes. His words brought a short silence upon the company.

Then Doon raised his voice again. "May King. You must know many tales, old and new. Can you tell us tales in the evenings?"

"Give us news of the world!"

"Sing the new songs."

Gawain muttered, "Sing, I cannot. Tell, aye. I can do that." Why not?

Merry's eyes popped open. "You forget," he told the men, "the May King works in the evenings."

"Ei. Ech. Aye!" Nods, winks, and digs.

"And we work many days."

Mock groans.

"But not all days. Next rain, come to our Men's House, May King, and give us a story."

"I will, if you call me by my name."

"Call you—what is it, Gawain?"

"Aye. This May King title grates on my ears."

The fellows murmured, "Gawain," trying it out.

One said loudly, "Look at the sun, Brothers!"

Men and boys looked up through beech leaves, sighed,

grunted, and found their feet. They stretched, peed, bent to pick up dropped scythes and hats.

"What!" Unpleasant surprise widened Gawain's eyes. "Is there more hay?" He had thought the field cut.

Merry swept an arm to point behind the beech shade.

There stretched another sun-drenched, wind-waved field.

God's eyes! Gawain had been ready to drift into sleep. His back, arms, and calves groaned. Satan's balls! Another endless field?

Merry touched his shoulder. "May King—"

Gawain growled.

"Gawain. You need not scythe."

Merry tilted his head and half smiled like . . . why, like Lady Green's troublesome little girl! "No need to work. After all, you are the—"

"God's blood, I'm coming! Coming. Now. I only didn't . . ."

Merry picked his straw hat off the ground and crowned Gawain with it. The yokels cheered.

"ME MYSELF," GRANNY SAYS. "In truth. One time I fell in love."

The softened wet reed cuts my finger. I lick blood and wave the finger in air to dry. At my feet, old Brindle Dog whines sympathy. Ynis lets her reed-braid drop to her knee as though she can't braid and listen at the same time. In truth, she can't.

Cross-legged, we sit around the tub of soaking reeds outside our hut. Nearby, our low fire hisses, waiting to fry Ynis's favorite honey cakes. We braid reeds, stitch the braids together, and toss small new mats on our growing pile. Ynis's mats show bumps, ridges, knots, and blood spots. Her small hands are bloodied as though she braided brambles.

"Aye, me myself!" Granny asserts again. "I fell in love. You'd never guess with who."

I joke. "I hope with Grandpa, Granny."

"Him? Nah! A good husband he was, dear, never a word against him. I truly loved that good man. But I weren't in love with him, you know how I mean."

"I dunno how you mean, Granny." Ynis cocks her head. Her little ears fairly twitch with curiosity.

"Pick up your reeds, Ynis."

"How do you mean?"

"That one's too big for the others. Get one the same size. Like that.

"I mean, dear, like when you can't live without him. He's all you think of. All day you wait for night, and him."

"Ech," says Ynis. "Yech. Ick."

"Wait a while, you'll change that tune! Anyhow, guess who I fell for flat on my face?"

Eyes on my work: "You'll have to tell, Granny."

Granny lowers her voice so the near neighbors at their reed tub won't hear. "I fell for the May King!"

My fingers freeze on the braid. I look up.

Our little fire wavers and sinks into ash. A giant bat-shadow swoops and hovers over us. I know the neighbors cannot see it. We four see it clearly. Ynis drops her work again. Trembling, Brindle tries to creep under my stool and twists himself into my dress. Granny braids on, squinting up uneasily at the hovering cloud. Maybe she should say no more.

But she goes on. "I were May Queen that year. He came from over Holly Wood way. He was the most love-some . . ." Granny sighs.

My mother died when I was born. This May King was a memory when she was born. But he lives today in Granny's heart. "He laughed a lot. I always did like a laughin' fellow."

"So." Does she guess? Does she see into my heart? Maybe she's just woolgathering, wandering in memory. "What did you do, Granny?"

"Do? What did I do . . . Ah, yes." With an effort she pulls herself out of dream. "First thing I did, I conceived his son. My first child."

So that son was my handsome uncle—the one who wed, fathered four handsome children, then died, with two of them, of a pox.

"Nextly, I prayed."

"And the Gods answered?"

"A Demon answered."

Ynis's small, soft mouth drops open. Her eyes follow Granny's words into air. She seems to see the words up there in the dark cloud, fluttering like moths.

"This Demon, he promised me gifts if I'd forget my May King. Wunnerful gifts. Powers. Till then I didn't have none. He gave me powers like so." Granny turns and points at the fire. The ashes spring to life. Flame licks up from air.

Ynis breathes, "What else, Granny?"

"Ech . . . he gave me the healing touch. I've lived well on that ever since. Many's the wart I've cured." But not the pox. "An' the seein' eye. That sees fairies an' auras an' hearts."

All that! "But I see too, Granny. Fairies and clouds."

"Aye. You two was born gifted. Not me."

All those gifts for turning from love! Keeping my eyes low so as not to see our dark cloud, I try to braid reeds again.

"I see that black cloud up there." Ynis points up at it. "I don't like that. Gives me the creepies."

31

"It'll go. If we talk somethin' else. Like about braidin' mats—"

Hastily—"Granny, I seed a thing last night. A big thing."

"Aye?"

"I came out here to pee."

"Use the pot, child. Nights, stay inside. Unless we're out here with you."

"This tree came walkin' by."

"Eh?"

Again my fingers freeze on the braid.

"Ech! It was like a beech tree, Granny. Branches swayin' 'round." Ynis waves arms, bobs head. "Feet stompin'—"

"You mean, roots."

"Nay, this tree it had feets. An' they shook the ground."

Granny mumbles, "Holy Gods! You were dreamin'."

"Nay, I were peein'."

"I guess it didn't notice you." Or you might not sit here now.

"It stomped right on by there." Ynis points to the neighbor's hut. Carefully, we do not look there. That would invite neighborly conversation.

"Whuff!" Granny exhales relief. "You were right lucky, Ynis. You were downright blessed. Like I say—nights, use the pot!"

I whisper to Ynis, "You saw the Green Man."

"Ma, I saw a tree!"

"Hush! Whisper. The Green Man looks like a tree. Or like a man. Or like grass. He is the life of trees, grass, men."

Granny whispers, "He walks now in summer. Winters, he lies in his grave. Spring, he up and rises again."

"He stomps and dances through the world. He blesses all crops. All weeds and woods."

"And us?"

"He blesses us through the crops," I explain. "We eat the crops and turn them into us. All that lives is really grass, Ynis. Grass magicked into flesh."

Ynis whispers, "He didn't look like blessin' to me. He gave me the creepies."

"So he should," Granny tells her earnestly. "He's mighty moody. He like to shred folk, be he in a mood."

I take this good chance to warn my child. "Spirits you see, Gods, Fairies, they are like folk. Not all good. Some downright bad. Some friendly. Some dangerous."

"Like I said," Granny puts in, "nights, use the pot! Ho, look how we've fallen behind here!" She turns and calls to the neighbors, "Hi! How many mats you made?"

I glance upward. Like smoke, our black cloud drifts away.

AN OWL CALLED FROM beyond the barley. Another answered from the far grove.

Gawain stretched, rolled over, and turned back to Lady Green. He drew her in toward him, edging his shoulder under her head. Her thick red hair spilled down his bare side and chest. Idly he lifted strands of it and wound them through his fingers, around his arms. He murmured, "You remind me of someone."

They lay under an awning between banks of pea plants. Reeds, branches, and whole saplings had been piled in rows and the peas planted to climb over the debris. Already the knee-high vines halfway covered the piles. Lady Green had pointed out the obvious virtue of their lovemaking. "The peas will be ready soon after Midsummer. They love your power, May King!"

He had reminded her. "Gawain, Love. Call me Gawain."

Quickly she promised, "I'll try to remember." He had only to ask and she, like all the rest, complied—except in the matter of a horse.

Now he said, "You remind me of someone . . . loved. I wish you did not."

She caressed his chest. "Why . . . Gawain? Does that not help you to love me?"

"It does. Therefore I wish not."

"You don't like . . . loving me?"

This love-talk irked Gawain. In truth, he did find himself almost loving Lady Green. Love came easily, as naturally as anger, to his eager, hungry heart. How could he help loving a woman who gave him so much pleasure every night? But honesty was more natural to him than love—and knightly as well.

So he said now, "Lady Green, I am going to leave you. We both know that."

"Aye, dear . . ."

"This loving of ours is only till Summerend. So I would like to love you less. Care less."

"Ungallant . . ."

"Aye, but truthful. Something in you calls out truth in me." That was not gallantry. Lady Green's direct gaze and uncompromising carriage did call from him the same honorable sincerity he practiced with men.

Chuckle. Snuggle. "Maybe I remind you of a former lover."

"No."

"Have you had so few you can be sure?"

"I have not been a great lover, Lady Green. Not like some of my brother knights." Maybe if he had been more practiced he would not now feel so tempted toward love.

"But you are talented. For instance—"

"No." He caught and held her hand. "Not now. If I could only remember, know, who it is you bring to mind . . ."

"Maybe we were lovers earlier."

"What earlier?"

"In another life."

"What?"

"You must remember living before."

"What!"

"Don't you dream sometimes of another life?"

"Oh, dreams. Haw! In dreams I can be anyone, any time, any age! In dreams I have been a tree . . . a young child . . . a stag. Once I even was"—he whispered this one—"a woman!"

"Because in the past, in other lives, you were such."

"Never! Lady Green, do you not know that we go to God in heaven when we die?"

"Maybe for a while. But then we long to see the warm green earth again, and we come back. You and I may have loved many times since the Goddess birthed the world."

"This I never heard or dreamed!"

"Or we may have been brother and sister. Or brother and brother. I dream I'm a man sometimes."

Owls called back and forth from field to grove to river. Gawain drew Green's hair across him like a blanket. "Let's dream now together that this fantasy of yours is solemn truth." A harmless game. "Do you think we could ever have been enemies, Lady Green?"

"Ech, aye! Maybe once we faced each other in battle; and now again, in love. We meet over and over again. Those we value in this life we have known before."

"Where did you hear this?"

"We know in our hearts. Everyone knows."

"Not where I come from!"

"That does not surprise me. Where you come from folk walk on their heads!"

"Seriously, Lady Green; not gaming, now. Our Faith teaches that we live but once in this world."

"Once? Once only?" She raised on her elbow to look down on him. "But who could leave this green world forever? Do you not love the world, May King? Gawain?"

"I am talking here of Truth, not love!"

"Are they different?"

He sat up beside her. "Lady Green! Gwyneth! The Truth is what God makes. Love is . . . love is only what we feel about what God makes."

"And that doesn't matter?"

"How could it matter? What is, is." Pools of earnest darkness, their eyes met in new moonlight. "I love you now," Gawain murmured. "But soon I must leave you. That is Truth. Even so we love the world, but we must leave it. That is Truth."

Lady Green shuddered. Moon-pale, she whispered, "But we belong to the world. With the Green Man we rise, flower, fruit, die, rise. The world and we are one."

"No!" Gawain told her firmly. "Trees and beasts belong to the world. God makes us human folk of body and soul. Our body returns to the world. But our spirit flies to God. If we have lived right."

Her wide, dark eyes drank in his words. "How do we live right, Gawain?"

"We follow God's law."

"God's law is the world's law."

"No, no. God has revealed His law to His prophets and priests. We listen to them. They teach us how to live."

"You talk now of human teaching. Human words."

"Our priests know God's words."

"We are God's words."

How to convince her?

They stared at each other, silent, while owls conversed.

Lady Green lay down first and patted the mat beside her. "Lie down, May King—Gawain." Carefully, he let himself down an arm's reach away. "This is no time or place for talk," she said. "We don't want the peas to hear us."

Nor the Green Man, she thought. *Neither!* She imagined him stomping angrily toward them through the peas, waving wild arm-branches, and she trembled.

Gawain snorted softly. "Lady Green, the peas hear nothing. Know nothing. Feel nothing. *They are only peas.*"

She murmured, "They are life, Gawain. Our life."

"Very well." He sighed in exhaustion. "But I can do nothing more for them right now."

"Sleep, Love."

He rolled away from her.

"I'll get your ale." She reached out toward the skin bottle, never far away.

"No ale."

"But—"

"Sleep now." He rolled away from her. He lay limp.

The small argument had roused him. In the new moonlight she had seen his eyes too conscious. His words had come too fast and feelingly.

Ech, he would go nowhere now. Sleep was as good for him as ale.

There. He snored.

Softly she sat back up. Then she reached behind her. Her searching fingers found the ale bottle, then a fold of silk.

Much earlier, Gawain had unlaced her green gem-crusted girdle and tossed it aside like any rag. A good thing he had not ripped it off her! Even when his square, strong fingers touched magic, this ignorant man felt it not.

She breathed apology to the girdle. "Ech, he meant nothing by it. He knows nothing. But had I worn you, I

37

would have known the words to calm him. Come now. Shield my heart."

She laced the girdle about her sturdy waist. Her whirling thoughts cleared and stilled.

She saw now a door opened before her into Gawain's mind. She saw the source of his pride, his stiff uprightness. "Our spirit flies to God, if we have lived right."

Ech! The man thinks he knows the World's mind!

When he holds me in his arms and knows not even my mind!

(And I. Do I know my own mind?)

His Faith teaches that we live but once in this world. But once.

She shuddered.

Death is the end for him. He thinks that once he dies he will never see Green Earth again. Holy Gods! Every morning he wakes to that thought. And yet he smiles and drinks all day and loves all night!

Foolish and ignorant he may be. But this is the bravest man I may ever know!

She leaned to caress his rumpled dark hair, his slack, sleeping shoulder.

I wish now I had not learned his mind. But it was already too late for me. Already I knew him as a man, not only as a tool ready for my hand.

Hoo! an owl called from the river.

Hoo-hoo! one answered from the barley.

"HOHO, GWYNETH!"

A lithe figure breaks from the crowd of men and strides jauntily across Fair-Field.

I haul Ynis's little tunic up out of the river, wring it out and toss it on the bank. My friends laugh and jibe before bending to their own wash again.

Barefoot and wet-gowned, I splash up on land. I would catch up my gown and run, limping through briars, but mature dignity forbids. I walk to meet him.

Smiling like summer itself, he comes to me. He cocks his head at me—Ynis's same gesture—and takes my hands.

"You're thinner," is all he says.

"Ech, Merry! Summertime. Much ado."

"You're pale."

"You've been watching me!"

"Surprised?"

His sweet calm shames me.

This is the real Merry, my first love. I knew this Merry before he went to turn druid—before he learned to make his face a mask and his very body a costume. Uneasily I face him now, with my spirit newly masked. I glance over his shoulder. "There goes the wheel!"

He slips his arm about my waist and turns to look. "We had to mend it. Last year it got fairly banged and burned."

"Next time you'll need to make a new one."

"Maybe right now. That's what we're finding out."

The huge, red-painted Sun-wheel rolls and bounces. Shouting fellows run to shove it, shore it up, poke it along with staves. "Seems to be holding together."

Older men push handcarts of wood toward the stone circle where soon the Midsummer Fire will roar. "Looks like the show's coming together."

"Better than ever, Gwyn. You won't believe the Green Men!"

"Then maybe you should try again."

He laughs. "I mean, you *will* believe the Green Men!" He sobers. "Gwyn. I know you. I suspect you."

39

"Suspect me?"

"You know how I mean."

"I could never fool you, Merry."

"It's hard for you." He squeezes my waist. "Truth, I like the fellow myself."

"You know him at all?"

"Oh, aye. He comes to work with us when he's bored. And he's going to knight the lot of us."

"What?"

"We're going to be the Square Table. Like King Arthur's Round Table. He'll teach us that show."

"Hmmm. I think you'll need ponies for that."

"In truth. But we'll watch him."

They surely will.

"We don't mean to go hungry, come winter. We'll take good care of him."

My arm steals around Merry's supple waist.

The careening Sun-wheel hits a bump and bounces high. Somebody gives it a good thwack from the other side, and it veers toward us. I hear my friends in the river squawk and splash.

"Wager you." Merry's lips touch my ear. "It'll go left." Suddenly hard, his arm holds me still.

The wheel reels at us. The yelling fellows "guiding" it do not see us. They care only that it hit the river, still wavering upright. We can still scuttle out of the way.

My arm tightens around Merry. I whisper through his curls, "I wager it'll go right."

It rolls at us.

Midsummer Eve, the Sun-wheel will be decked in flame. Torches stuck through its center will stream fire as it rolls, reels, and bounds to the river. Folk will grab children out of its way. Young couples will dash across its track, the closer the merrier. Hurt and harm may well happen.

Here it comes rumbling by daylight, grim and fireless.

Merry squeezes my waist. With his other hand he points the wheel left. If I point right, the confused wheel may plough us under. I point left too. "Left!" We both shout to the advancing wheel.

Maybe one of the guides sees us. I think not. I think the wheel sees us. It hops and turns left. It rolls by us an arm's length away. The running guides stomp our toes as we step back.

Shrieks from the river. We turn to see women, girls, and children scatter. Some climb the bank, some swim out deeper.

The Sun-wheel totters through their midst. It poises a moment on the brink. Leaning, it spins halfway around. With a final poke and a great splash it dives in.

Cries of relief from the women. Growls from the guides.

As hunters come to their killed quarry, so the guides come to the bank and look down.

We still hold each other. Merry breathes, "It's dead."

"Broke up."

"There's just time to make a new one."

We still stand tight-locked. Deliberately I loosen my arm on his waist. My cheek brushes his shoulder. "Hey, Merry. What did we think we were doing?"

"Gaming?"

"We didn't even wager anything."

"No time to think."

Gravely I tell him, "A Demon made us do it."

He laughs and loosens up. We let each other go.

Midsummer night.

Gawain watched out for Merlin.

Green-crowned again and freshly dressed in new white linen, he led the dance around the rising fire with Lady Green. This time the crown stayed tight to his head, where she had fastened it. He twirled and kicked and leaped, hand in hand at first with Lady Green, later with others. At one point he found himself gently whirling Old Lady Granny. Once he snatched little Ynis off her feet and swung her flat out. But she did not shriek with joy as other children did. Swung arcing around, unsmiling, she kept serious eyes on his face. He was glad to pass her along and take on a fat matron from another village.

Lady Green had told him that three villages met at this Midsummer Fire. Here he saw again the white-bearded old druid who had crowned him May King. He stood a little aside from the action, holding a leafy staff upright as though planted. Gawain noticed that the dancing, jostling throng left a quiet island around him.

Breathing hard between dances, Gawain watched out for Merlin.

Late at night, masked and antlered Green Men cavorted out from the dark sacred grove. They leaped like stags, waving and jabbing at bystanders with hawthorn staves. And among them, yet carefully apart, staggered trees: huge towers of branches, leaves, flowers, and ribbons.

Pipe music that had never paused since sundown quavered to silence. Drums thumped on, louder at each thump till Gawain felt them inside his own chest, stronger than his heartbeat.

The crowd hushed and stilled to watch three trees dance. Slowly they whirled, close around the fire. Gawain thought it must be hard to see out from inside a tree, especially at night, fire on one side, dark on the other.

Of course there were men inside those trees. Those were human feet that stomped and thumped under their leaf-skirts.

Or were they?

Gawain's head swam with ale and dancing.

The Green Men were certainly masked men. But the dancing trees that swayed out from the dark sacred grove, guarded at a safe distance by their human servants . . .

He took Lady Green's hand and bent to whisper, "What are those trees?"

"As you say. They are trees."

"No, in truth. What, who, are they?"

"Tree-spirits, May—Gawain. Look how majestically they move!" Admiration flamed with fire-reflection in her eyes.

Drums beat in Gawain's blood. These three might be tree-spirits, for all he knew. They might be Demons, or savage Gods, or spirits of summer and time. Slowly he signed the Cross on brow, breast, and both shoulders. "Holy Mary," he breathed. "Angel Michael . . ."

Only when the trees stomped back into the grove—that same finger of grove from which Gawain had first ventured onto Fair-Field—only then did the drums soften and the pipe music rise again. The crowd relaxed and smiled. Gawain took Green's hand to lead the dance again. But first, quickly, he scanned the crowd, watching out for Merlin.

Green had said Arthur's mage often came to Midsummer here in this field. Gawain planned to waylay him. Merlin might well not know him at all in his savage outfit and flower crown, beard untrimmed, thin from travel and travail. Gawain would block Merlin's path and announce himself. (With inward glee he imagined Merlin's stuttering astonishment. He would learn that he and his fellows were not the only ones who could amaze!) Then Gawain would offer himself as Merlin's escort home to Arthur's Dun. "That is, Mage, if you can wrangle me a horse from these stubborn bumpkins" . . . which Merlin would do with a word mumbled in the headman's ear before morning.

From May Day to Midsummer had been a diverting adventure. And Lady Green, Gwyneth, had been surprisingly alluring for a savage peasant girl. But now Gawain was more than ready to go home to himself and his world.

Quickly he glanced around the firelit crowd for a slightly stooped, white-haired figure bearing a harp like a shield on his shoulder. Maybe talking with the white-bearded druid no one talked with?

No. No Merlin, anywhere.

Later, fellows of the Square Table upended a great red wheel. They lit torches from the Midsummer Fire and poked them into holes in the center. Then with shouting and drum-rolls they beat the flaring wheel like a huge hoop toward the river. God save whoever got in its way!

The crowd screamed joyful excitement. When the wheel crashed into the river, men leaped like hares and threw their children in the air. Old fellows waved canes, young girls loosened gowns.

Thirsty Gawain quaffed ale from Green's bottle. He told her, "All this reminds me of something. As if I'd been here before."

She arched surprised eyebrows. "They don't celebrate Midsummer at Arthur's Dun?"

"Not like this." He seemed to remember that all this dizzy noise was meant to encourage the sun. But Christians knew that only God ruled the sun. "Peasants do something like this." Gawain was not sure what exactly they did.

Green took back her bottle and stored it under her gown. "Now it's time to jump the fire."

"What!"

Green grasped his hand. "It's low enough. Over here. Come on, they're all waiting for us to lead."

Hand in hand, Gawain and Lady Green ran at the low line of fire and jumped. It seemed to Gawain that he jumped straight into dying flame. But Green's hand lifted him. His feet found cool earth again.

The yokels roared approval. Turning, Gawain saw young couples running and leaping where they had run and leaped.

Green squeezed his hand. "Now we go."

"Go?" That now familiar ale-fuzz muffled thought.

"To the grove. Now, while they're all watching the jumps."

"The grove? But that's where . . ." That's where the dancing trees had gone. He had no wish to meet one of those.

"That's where we work our magic, May King." She drew him away, out of the crowd.

Groping into grove darkness, Gawain asked Green, "Where was Merlin? I was . . . were . . . I watched for Merlin . . ."

"Why?"

"Had something to tell him. Ask him. He weren't . . . wasn't there."

She laughed. "Merlin is not the sun, Gawain. He does not come and go at sacred times. He's only human."

"Think he'll come later?"

"He'll come when he wants to, May King."

"Gawain, girl. Gawain."

"I meant to say Gawain. Dear Gawain."

GRANNY SAW INTO MY heart. To warn me, she told us her sad story, how long ago she loved her May King. Gods! She loves him still. Love lit her old eyes as she spoke of him.

I heard her. But already by then I couldn't help myself.

Look at him, Gwyneth! Sit up here beside him and look upon those straight, brave brows, those feeling, firm lips, sleep-slacked now. Who could look without love?

Such a brave child he is!

And I. Am I not brave too?

New sunlight steals down through oak leaves and through my thinning thatch. Mist curls past and into my open bower door. Something moves in the mist. I grasp Gawain's shoulder and cling. Heart beats a small drum-roll. Body-eyes see only mist.

Spirit, unfold yourself! Rise into your own space, see in your own light.

Frightened Spirit folds and curls itself low in my stomach. Something moves nearer in mist.

Under my stiff-frozen hand Gawain's shoulder turns cold. I cannot lift my hand, or draw frozen breath to cry, "Gawain, defend me!" Which how could he do? I sit here encased in ice, entirely alone.

A voice not my own speaks inside my head. It creaks and stumbles, as Gawain's voice did when he first came to us out of the grove. He told me he had not spoken in days. Likewise this voice speaks not often, nor easily. Inside my head it clears throat, licks lips. It says, *Give to us, Gwyneth. We pay.*

A good thing I need not speak aloud! Ice closes my throat.

What do you pay?

What you want?
I want . . . I want power.
Aha. Power. What power you got now, Gwyneth?
You know. You know all.
Not all. Tell.
I have . . . I see ghosts. Auras.
Don't see us!
No. I don't see you yet.
Wanna see?
Ah. Ech. No. I think I need not see you.
Wise Gwyneth. You got prophecy?
I read the future in stones.
Nah, naaah! Prophecy in heart. Look. See. Know.
I don't do that.
You will.
What?
You give us ours. We pay prophecy.
Gawain stirs under my hand. I glance down at him. He
rolls his head toward me, his eyelashes strive to lift—long
black eyelashes, lovely as a girl's.
That one. Give us that one, Gwyneth.
Why do they ask and bargain? *What choice have I?*
Bitterly, *Always choice.*
Always choice . . . when I thought I had none . . .
Gawain's mouth drops open as in horror. His dear
grey eyes startle wide, then narrow and droop. His ruddy
face greys, then greens; Gawain's dear head seems severed
from its sturdy neck.
You give. We pay. Your choice.
Eyes on Gawain's dead face, I strive to move. With
huge effort I lift my hand from his shoulder, reach out
behind me, grasp my green silk girdle. It burns my hand.
Hah! No need. We go.
I draw the warm, protecting girdle about my waist.
Your choice, Gwyneth.

47

The voice dies away out of my head. Empty, innocent mist curls past and into my open bower door. The girdle's warmth spreads through me, from stomach to breasts, down arms and legs. Gawain's face turns from green to grey to ruddy. Under closed lids, life fills out his eyes.

Prophecy. They pay prophecy.

Choice. I have choice.

ALE MUG AT HAND, Gawain rested in Old Lady Granny's hut. Light rain splattered the thatch close above him. Then it paused. Rain had come and gone, heavy and light, all this cool, sleepy day. Gawain had passed the morning in Men's House, telling Round Table tales to the fascinated Square Table. Now toward evening he stretched out alone on Lady Granny's floor mats, embroidered down cushions propping up head and shoulders. He drank and dreamed.

"May Queen, that's me," a child's harsh voice declared close behind his head, just outside. "Gimme them flowers."

"Aaaah!" another child disagreed. "Maevis. I vote for Maevis."

"We don't vote," the first voice decided. "I'm May Queen. And May King, that's . . ."

"Alvie! Eddy! Hearny!" Children squealed. A dog barked—Granny's friendly old Brindle.

Gawain's heavy eyes opened. Had he dreamed? He stared up into the arched branches that roofed Granny's hut. From the highest arch swung pots, brushes, small tools for various tasks—mysteries to Gawain—and clean ceremonial garments. Three long green gowns hung up there, with loops of green jewelry and strings . . . and strings . . . and strings of true-gold rings.

Gawain's eye rested thoughtfully on dim-shining bracelets and strung rings. He had not been dreaming. Just outside the thatch behind him real children played a real game. Rain could not confine them indoors.

The first, imperious voice said, "May King's Brucie."

Protests. "Too little. Too ugly. Too dumb."

"Ech! *You* don't want to be May King, do you?"

Mumbles.

"So. Gimme that there crown. Let me put this on you, Brucie . . ."

Brucie squawked. Gawain imagined the smallest boy outside squirming as the flower crown descended. He gave a small remembering squirm himself.

Brindle barked. Gawain could almost see his tail swing.

"Music!" the bully demanded. And music commenced—what sounded like a broken-pot drum, several quavering reed pipes, and children whistling.

Gawain sat up, dizzy. (More and more often he woke up dizzy.) He drained the mug beside him.

"This here's the maypole. Come on, Brucie. We lead." One by one, dancing children quit whistling. The reed pipes and drum kept up a fairly lilting rhythm.

Gawain rose to his knees, stretched, yawned. Tried the mug again. Not a drop left in it.

"Ynis, let's stop. That's plenty there. We gotta breathe."

Ynis! Gawain should have known that determined, unchildish voice!

But he had never seen Ynis play with other children. He had thought they rejected her company, as he would like to do himself. Here she was, not only playing but commanding the play, and the others caved in before her like peasants before a queen.

"Oh, very well." The ragged music ceased. "We can't do

Midsummer. So it's Summerend now. Get the scythe, Con."

Scythe? Gawain let the mug fall. With both hands he laid hold of the thatch beside him and pulled apart a peep-hole.

Just outside, green-clad, flower-crowned Ynis pointed commandingly to Granny's chopping block. Two quite big boys laid hold of little flower-crowned Brucie. They plunked him down on his knees in a puddle beside the block.

Brucie wailed. Brindle swung his tail and whined. The gang of children stood around panting.

Here through their midst came Con, white-robed like a druid in a man's worn-out tunic. In both hands he held a scythe. A real scythe.

"Wait!" Ynis stopped Con in his tracks with a raised palm. "You want oak leaves on that scythe."

"Oak leaves!" Con growled and swung the scythe carelessly. Children close by jumped aside.

That was a real scythe. Sharp. Oak leaves or no. Brucie wailed from the chopping block where the big boys held his head down. Brindle lifted his head and howled.

Gawain saw himself the only adult in sight. With an effort he gathered his wits. Stood up. Pushed aside the leather-hinged door and glared down at the children. "In the name of holy Christ and Mary, what do you think you're doing?"

Small wet faces gaped up at him. Even Ynis betrayed surprise.

"Con, you better get that scythe back before it's missed. Run. Scat, you. All of you." Gawain waved at the gang as Lady Granny would wave at flocking chickens.

Squawking children scattered. An older girl ran the sobbing Brucie away. His wet flower crown dripped, abandoned, on the chopping block.

"Except you." In two strides Gawain grabbed Ynis's wrist. Reed-thin, it seemed to crumble in his fist. He shifted his hold to the shoulder of her drenched green tunic. Confused Brindle growled, then wagged.

"God's teeth, Girl! What evil game do you play?"

She raised a calm face to him. Her flower crown never slipped. Like her ma, she knew how to fasten it, even in wet hair. "May Day. We was just playin' May Day."

"May Day with a scythe?" He shook her.

"Couldn't do Midsummer. You need a fire for Midsummer."

"So?"

"So it's rainin'."

He shook her more fiercely. "The scythe?"

"So we skipped to Summerend."

Summerend. Summerend?

"Listen, you Girl. You don't play with real scythes."

"Brucie wouldn't get hurt. Con's his brother."

"Hah! A lot you know about brothers!" Quick, broken memories of his own brothers flashed across Gawain's mind. "Next May Day game, pretend a scythe."

She sighed.

Dizzy, mazed, he stared down into her quiet eyes. "Pretend a Midsummer Fire too." No telling what these wild brats might do!

"Have to," she agreed. Her flower crown nodded. "If it rains."

And now came real rain, hard into her upturned face.

GAWAIN AWOKE.

He came wide awake lying on his side, staring into clear white moonlight.

That's the door of Lady Green's bower, he thought. *She left it open.*

He reached around behind him on the pallet and found it empty. *She's gone out and left the door open.*

Close by, an owl hooted.

Gawain sat up slowly, to avoid dizziness. This time it did not come. *Not dizzy. Head clear.*

Remembrance flooded in.

Drank no ale yesterday. Dribbled it all on the ground when she wasn't looking. Why?

That ale of hers is spiked.

His deep mind spoke up. *Come, Sir! Up and out of here. Let's find what we can see ourself, with no lovely Lady Green at our elbow.*

Perfectly awake, Gawain rose, stooped under the low-arched roof. He ducked through the bower doorway and out among the half-moonlit oaks.

An owl called quickly twice from just above him. Another answered twice from the river.

Here we are, at last by ourself. Which way, Sir?

Gawain considered. North lay the pasturelands where herds wandered, guarded by youngsters with packs and tents, on their own for the first time. *Like us, Sir!*

Northeast stretched the Fair-Field and mowings. East, over the shallow river, flourished the crops whose growth Gawain and Lady Green encouraged.

She's never let you go south.

Lady Green said that south was sacred grove, then

deeper and more sacred grove. She said that nobody goes south.

Maybe that's for us!

Gawain considered this uneasily. A feeling he did not care to call fear prickled his stomach. *I think not this time.*

He found himself moving northwest. An owl hooted above him. Two far owls answered. Gawain stopped short, hand on oak trunk.

Those aren't owls. Those are sentries.

Inner Mind commented. *You are right, Sir. Notice now that wherever you move, an owl signals.*

I am a prisoner.

Aye.

God's teeth! What do they want? Do they plan to attack King Arthur and fear I might warn him?

Let us not joke, Sir.

Gently, Gawain stepped northeast from oak shade to moonlight to oak shade. Sure enough, hooting owls kept pace, and once a twig snapped nearby.

I've been half asleep since I came here. It's that helldamned ale she gives me. But, God's bones, what can they want?

Little Ynis said in his head, "We couldn't do Midsummer." Midsummer was now well past.

"So we skipped to Summerend."

Summerend.

Gawain came to an edge of grove. He glanced up at the moon. How long now till Summerend? He stood on a rise looking out over the moor.

Long, long ago he had stood like this on a cold cliff looking over a cold, moonlit sea. A calm voice overhead had said, "At Summerend, the Old Ones cut the May King down like the crops. They gave his blood to the Goddess." Little Gawain had shivered.

"We don't do that now," the voice continued. "Now we

sacrifice a straw man, a John Barleycorn. But in the old days the blood was real."

His mother, Morgause, had stood over Gawain, a tower between him and a fierce north wind. Her dark cloak blew about his back. Fascinated, he had asked, "How did they cut him down?"

"They cut off his head with a scythe. Like the crops."

Gawain stood now rooted, staring over moonlit moor instead of moonlit sea. *God and Mary shield!*

That's it, Sir. Your eyes open at last.

The old ways still lived in this God-forgotten north!

You remember the fellow they were going to crown May King when you came along? Remember his face, how miserable? And then how happy, when they crowned you instead!

"God's blood!" Gawain murmured aloud as his own blood congealed in his veins.

Hush, Sir. The guard might hear. Let them think you're still drugged out of your skull.

Must get out of here!

Truly, Sir. But how?

Must think how.

Drink no more ale, Sir.

That wretched girl! That Delilah! I'll strangle her with her own rich red hair!

Not yet, Sir.

Far out on the white moor something moved. Something moon-large, moon-white.

That's a horse, Sir.

Too big. All they've got here is rough little northern ponies.

That's a knight's charger.

It is! Big as my own Warrior that the savages ate. Angel Michael, that's what I need! If I could catch that horse—

Someone else has.

The great white horse ambled closer through white moonlight. A figure sat upright on its back. Two figures.

That's a woman, Sir. With a child before her.

She rode easily, swaying erect, guiding the charger apparently with heels and thighs. Gawain saw no sign of reins.

My mother told me once of a Goddess of horses. Maybe this . . .

Goddess? Or ghost, on a ghost horse? Gawain prickled. His tongue swelled fuzzily to fill his mouth.

Come, Sir! You've been thinking too much about the past. That's a real woman out there with a real child, on a real horse. And they're really too far to catch.

Disgustedly, Gawain shook himself. He spit out fear. *God's teeth! I'm crazed. I've been crazed since May Day.*

You've been drunk-drugged.

True. Now I'm clear, must stay clear. I've wits enough, strength enough, to escape from here.

In truth, Sir!

I am a Christian. Angels and Saints will aid me.

Very true.

I am Sir Gawain, King's Companion! If I but keep my head, no northern savages can hold me.

Right, Sir. Keep your head and keep your head.

I'll escape. And Merlin shall sing of my adventure.

The great moon-white horse paced slowly out of sight into deep moonlight.

THE SQUAT, ROUGH-COATED PONY shied away from the joust.

Gawain cursed, clapped heels to hide, beat rump with awkwardly gathered reins. The pony changed its untrained mind. Gawain barely had time to aim "lance" and heft "shield" before the pony bore him, bouncing, into battle.

The Square Table roared and clashed. Half-wild ponies reared and plunged. Men whacked and thwacked with "lances" (peasant cudgels); "shields" dropped unheeded and were broken under-hoof. Knaves struck each other down, leaped down themselves, and wrestled. Snarling, they lost themselves in crazy rage like fighting dogs. It was by Merry's good thought that they bore no knives, no weapons but the ungainly "lances."

Even so, Gawain did damage.

As he reeled almost helplessly bareback, young Doon charged him. Gawain aimed his "lance" square at the on-coming face. He fully expected the boy to raise his shield. To his surprise, his "lance" crashed square into an aston-ished, unprotected face. Gawain felt the hard, familiar jolt.

Heels over head, Doon went down over his pony's tail.

Gawain rode on through the melee, clashing cudgels with all he met, toppling many to the ground.

Reaching open, uncluttered space he managed to turn the bucking pony. Behind him his challengers found their feet, alone or with help. Ponies bucked loose and galloped away. Men grinned and joked even as they limped.

Gawain gave a quick glance southward, over the open fields. He imagined himself beating the pony into a gallop. He imagined the Square Table thundering after him, "lances" aloft. Slowly, he rode back into their midst.

A hand caught his rein. Merry looked up at him so-berly. He said, "Doon's hurt bad. Come see."

Merry led the sidestepping, bridling pony back to the boy on the ground. Doon's friends moved aside to let Ga-wain look down on the damage.

Dark young Doon held a fresh-torn rag over his left eye. He rocked back and forth and around and moaned to hurt his friends' ears. They glared up at Gawain.

He slid down from the pony. Better not stand out above the crowd like a straw-man target. "He's alive, God-thank!"

"No thanks to you, May King," one man growled.

Merry said fairly, "We knew this jousting could jar us."

Another man spat past Gawain's boot toe. "The eye's out, Merry."

"Holy Gods."

"If this stranger weren't the May King—"

"But he is, Bert."

"Aye," men murmured, nodding around Gawain. "Aye, he'll get it back. We'll see him get it back, ayah."

Clearheaded, Gawain understood their jargon. They would rejoice to see Doon's eye avenged at Summerend. Gawain straightened tall. He said sincerely, "Holy Mary! I did not mean for that." (Or did he? He was angry enough with all these murderous yokels!) "But you could hardly hope to joust without injury. I struck too truly. But I expected him to shield himself."

Merry said again, "We all knew jousting was chancy. You and you, get Doon safe home. I'll see him there later. May King, what does the Round Table do after an accident like this?"

"Why, the joust goes on."

"Ech, ayah. What I thought. Back at it, men!"

That morning Gawain learned what to expect of the Square Table. They were savages, fierce and brave, but untrained. They had no notion how to ride and fight at the same time. They did one or the other. The use of saddles, stirrups, and spurs would much aid their horsemanship. But Gawain was not the man to tell them that. Pitted against the Round Table, they would offer no contest. No contest against a bunch of squires!

And he himself, rightly a-horse, could doubtless fight off the lot of them.

"WHAT? WHAT CAN YOU mean, May King?"

"I know why you won't use my name." Quietly, dully, he says this. Quiet, dull dread echoes his voice in my bones.

"Gawain. What do you mean, you will not love me? Am I less lovely than before?"

"No less. Maybe more." Moonlit, his dark eyes glint.

We sit under our awning between pea rows, knees touching. Eagerly, my body yearns toward him. In the act of unloosing my girdle, I lean over and slide its soft silk along his furry chest. This gesture has always stirred him. Till now. Now he pushes girdle and hand roughly away. Leaning forward, he challenges me with his eyes.

Mind shines in his eyes. Ah! Too much mind, much too keen.

"Wait, love. I know what you need." I reach out for the bottle.

"No!"

"Eh?" Fingers pause on the bottle.

"Ale will I never drink again, till I come again under Arthur's reign."

"What? I remember this line, or one like it, from one of Merlin's stranger songs. "You will not drink . . . Gawain, you are not yourself."

Till now, our May King has seemed a simple enough fellow; brave, honest (not like me!), always ready to drink and love. In truth, many have marveled at his capacity for drink and love. Now I seem to be looking an entire other, unknown man in the face. Here is a time for slow caution, for feeling my way.

"Very well, May—Gawain. You need not drink. But love—"

"You I will never love again, till I love you under Ar-thur's reign."

I strain to see his aura. What shape, what color, flares around him now? If I could see that . . . but auras do not shine in the dark. All I see is his solid, beautifully male silhouette against stars.

"You have lost your senses."

"No, Lady Green. I have found them at length."

I reach out to touch him. Again he pushes my hand away.

Sitting here so close, my hungry body cries out for him. It is all I can do to not hurl myself upon him. "You don't want me to touch you?"

"I do not."

Can it be . . . can he . . . dare I ask?

I undo and shrug my green gown down about my waist. Now I dare. "Why? May—Gawain. My love. Why?"

"Let us be honest together, you and I."

"In truth! I have always—"

"You have not, Lady Green." Dry severity. As though he did not see my body hunger.

"You are ungallant . . ."

"No more games."

"Very well, Gawain. Be you honest with me."

"Very well, Lady Green. I must away, and that with all good speed."

"Away?" Step carefully here! "You know we need you here while the crops grow. After Summerend—"

"At Summerend I will be cut down with the crops."

A sentinel owl hoots over by the river. Women's soft voices murmur from the barley. Or are those the voices of startled, disappointed Fairies? Hope and desire sigh away in me to silence. I lift my gown again and secure it at the throat.

In his most formal, stilted language, Gawain says, "I

59

will drink none, love none, here in this place, Holy Oak. But in King Arthur's Dun I will take my fill of all good things. There, too, shall you take your fill."

"I? Never shall I see King Arthur's Dun." From what he has told me, I have no slightest wish to see it.

"If you wish, Lady Green, you shall see it as my bride."

"Bride," I repeat, slowly. "You mean, wedded wife?"

"I mean it so."

I know what that would mean in the south, in Arthur's Dun. He has told me.

"Lady Green, I swear to you by God, His angels and Saints, that when we come to Arthur's Dun we two shall be wed together, and we shall live together honorably till death."

"I must think on this."

"Think. But not too long."

Through the dark I feel the new hardness of his gaze as he watches me lace on my magic girdle. It warms my cold innards, stiffens my spine. "I will go from here, Gawain, and think."

"Go with blessings."

"You feel quite sure of me! How do you know I will not go straight to Merry?"

"Merry's the one in charge, as I thought."

"Aye."

"You will not go to him. You love me, Lady Green. Even as I love you."

In truth, in very truth, I do love him.

Coolly, I shrug, crawl out from under the awning, and depart.

I make for the grove—not for my bower, on the safer edge of grove, but for the forbidden, secret Shrine at the center. This dark trail is barely marked. Few walk it, and seldom. As we breathe unconsciously, never visiting the inner chambers of our body except in sickness, so the Tribe lives unconsciously around this Shrine, never visiting it except in great need.

Urgently, I seek counsel of the Gods whose presence I feel more strongly at every step.

Gawain spoke truth, back there under the awning. I do love him. Young Granny was no more fool than I! How can I give Gawain up now? I must save him.

Merlin sings a song about a pearl. *My pearl of price is past all price, All price I've paid and pain* . . . Which I always thought poetic folly. How could one pearl be past all price?

To save my love from sacrifice, I would need to sacrifice all that I have.

I would need to sacrifice my good and happy life. I never thought much of it before. For years I have taken high status and self-worth almost for granted. Only the serious thought of losing these, of traveling south, where I would be nothing more than a handsome woman—Gawain's woman, at that—only this thought brings my present good fortune clearly to mind.

Is Gawain my pearl of price?

To save him, I would need to sacrifice my Tribe. She, the Great Lady of barley, millet, peas, and onions, waits for his blood.

Would She forgive this unpaid debt? Unlikely. Maybe She could not forgive. Maybe Her power depends entirely on payment.

My Tribe's hunger might pay for my pearl.

I would need to leave Student Druid Merry behind forever—Merry, with his dancing step and bouncing curls; vigorous, magical Merry, whom I have almost promised to wed.

Even to think this, I must find Gawain a pearl of very great price!

Holy, dread Gods, I would need to abandon You!

Once gone south I would find myself under Arthur's rule and Gawain's, and that of their One God, who speaks through his priests and prophets.

Is Gawain my pearl of price, past all price? My body cries out, Aye! Aye! Aye! My soul looks on, appalled.

One price I will not pay. Even if I abandon Granny, Merry, my Tribe, my Gods, I will never abandon Ynis. Ynis will come south with us.

Unseeing in the dark, I step into water.

THE HOLY SPRING.

This spring rises out of the Goddess's own footprint, pressed into stone. I have stumbled into the stream that spring sends down through stone, fern, and bramble, to join the river.

This holy, sacred water flows direct from dread Shrine to everyday, useful river. We drink this water, we bathe in it and wash clothes in it. We weave our mats from the reeds it grows. In like manner, all our life flows from the Gods.

Ankle-deep in cold water, I hesitate. A cold wind seems to blow from the Shrine ahead; yet no breeze stirs a leaf.

Knee-deep a chill, not from the water, seizes my spine. Breath comes shallow.

Ankle-deep again, I feel my heart thud like a waking drum.

In these three steps I splash across the stream and enter the Shrine.

Moonlight falls brighter here, because here no trees but oaks grow; all undergrowth and othergrowth have been cleaned away. Moving through silver light, I touch each oak trunk as I pass. *Friend!* I breathe to each. *Guardian of Gods. Announce me. Tell Them I come in prayer and peace.*

The drum of my heart thuds dolefully. Breath and feet falter.

Crunch. I step on a long bone.

Undergrowth has been cleared away but not the scattered bones of God-feasts.

I reach to touch the next oak but draw back. Where I had thought to touch hangs a head.

Moonlit-green. Rotted. Gnawed by squirrels and pecked by birds, it glowers, lidless, down at me.

I do not touch that oak. The next one also bears a head. Most oaks this near the altar bear heads. In her time, Granny hung two of them.

If I do not help Gawain escape, come Summerend I will have to nail up his head, maybe on this very tree where I lean now, catching harsh breath.

I tell myself, *Nothing to fear from bones or heads. No human ghosts walk here.* All these spirits flew long ago to the Summerland, or as Gawain would say, to God. Maybe some have returned by now to walk our green earth in new forms. But they do not linger here.

Gods and Demons linger here.

Two trees ahead, moonlight glares on bare altar-stone.

Green earth is the Gods' house. We are Their bodies. They live everywhere, in everything. But Their presence in this place stops breath, freezes spine and skull.

Here in this Shrine lives the darkness of the Gods. Here live Demons who embody Death, Cruelty, and all-smiling Evil. Because darkness and terror are held here, circled by protecting oaks, Sun and Moon can shine.

At sight of the altar my heart booms. Only my magic girdle holds me up against the tree. My fingers seek the girdle, smooth it, pleat it.

63

I have come here to ask the question of my life. Here, the Gods will answer.

I push myself away from the tree. Hardly breathing, swaying as though drugged, I come to the altar.

It is a long, bare stone, waist-high. No moss grows on it. Lichen that dares to grow is scraped off. But no scraping, no rain, can clean the blood stains and streams that darken the stone.

Standing before this altar, I ask aloud: "What would You have me do?" And listen. I am prepared to listen here till morning. But the answer is immediate.

Not my ears, but my eyes, notice movement to the north. Moonlight walks among the oaks.

No. A white fallow doe walks among the oaks.

She is one of those magic white deer who watch over our Tribe. Their presence promises peace and safety. Maybe she is the very one who led Gawain to our Fair-Field on May Day. She ambles past across the altar from me, and after her trip two half-grown kids, white as herself.

Our magic white deer have grown rare of late. My thudding heart leaps to see these two white fawns skip and frolic. Abruptly, the doe stands. Side by side, still jostling, the kids stand. Six dark eyes stare at me across the altar. Six ears wiggle and stretch.

For generations, no one has disturbed the white deer of our oak grove. Now they are hardly even wild. I stretch out a greeting hand. Softly I tell them, "I am Gwyneth, asking a question."

The white doe twitches her tail.

"Do you bring me my answer?"

She snuffles.

"Show me my way, White Doe."

She stamps. Her kids look from me to her. She walks

away south. The kids follow, soberly, not playing now. South they go from moonlight into shadow and disappear.

I stand like a young tree, hand still outstretched. Could the Gods answer more clearly? The three magic deer promise safety to my Tribe. And they went southward—toward Arthur's Dun.

Inside my head, a rasping voice clears throat and croaks, *Prophecy, Gwyneth. We pay prophecy.*

I am a tree. My outstretched hand is a branch, my fingers twigs.

You want more? More. We pay . . . healing. Healing, too.

What . . . should I call you? (You, who live so quietly in my mind I did not guess your presence.)

Call us nothing.

You know my name. I would know yours.

You want, you give us name!

But what is the name of Evil?

Listen, Gwyneth. We prophesy you now. That one promise to wed.

Aye, he promised that.

That one lie. Will not wed.

Will not?

Lie to you. Make vain promise. Never wed.

I gasp. That slight motion frees my hand and loosens up my ragged breath.

You give us that one. We pay. Prophecy. Healing.

But . . . Holy Gods, a dreadful thought!

Would you live in me, then?

Hah! Live in you now.

My hand sinks to touch the altar.

Lightning shoots from fingertips up wrist and arm. I snatch my hand away.

Remember, Gwyneth. Give! Us! Ours!

Their voice rasps away to silence.

But now I know it has not gone far. It lies unknown in my mind, as a viper may lie unknown in thick thatch. I have clasped hands over heart, as though for defense. But there can be no defense from Those within. They may speak at any moment. Am I cursed? Or do They live in every heart?

Prophecy and healing They promise me—two gifts I have long sought.

Gawain promises love—a pearl past price?

About to move, to turn about and leave the altar, I draw deep breath. Something thuds among northward oaks, where the white deer came from. Twigs, or bones, crack.

What blunders out from the trees is so tall, so dark, I do not rightly see it until too late to move.

One oak steps out from the others. With slow, thudding steps it sways past, across the altar from me. If I leaned across the altar I could touch it. If it leaned to me across the altar . . .

I am a tree. My folded arms are branches, my fingers twigs. Slow as a tree I breathe, see, feel, so that the God has passed by me and gone His way before I see Him clearly. This way, I manage not to fall unconscious on the altar.

As you wake from a dream, remembering, so now I remember the God who paced by me a moment ago. His head was a huge ball of twigs and leaves, flower-crowned. His long, long arms were branches, swinging loose. The fingers, which could shred living bodies, seemed dry and delicate as thin sticks. Loose-swinging vines, sprouting unlikely flowers, robed His trunk.

Unbreathing, I watch Him stomp away south and disappear, dark among his rooted fellows.

South.

South.

MERRY PANTED, "DOON SAID you . . . came . . . to see him."

Gawain swung at Merry. "Couldn't very well not . . . I did put his eye out."

In Arthur's Dun, rich Gawain could have offered some recompense for Doon's lost eye. Here, as the condemned May King, he had nothing at all to offer. Yet Honor had compelled him to visit Doon's hut and assure the boy yet again that he had meant no harm.

"Was but . . . accident," Merry reminded him now.

"Aye. Watch out now, Merry. You want no accident yourself!"

"Fear not, I know you now!" Merry saluted with his wicker shield.

Their two ponies jostled each other unwillingly. With peasant cudgels, Gawain and Merry thwacked each other's shields. They were supposedly alone in the mowing. But Gawain had spotted two ponies tethered under trees, in which he guessed watchful guards hid. More guards might hide nearby.

Merry needed little instruction in swordplay. But the combination of sword and horse was new to him. Earnestly he dueled with one hand while reining with the other. Gawain himself found this not so easy bareback, on an untrained pony.

At first the "duel" needed all his attention. Besides turning and restraining the animal, he had to restrain himself and his untamed temper. Let there be no more accidents! Well he knew that if the savages did not wait for his blood at Summerend they would have shed it for Doon on the jousting field.

Thrust, parry, and rein came easier now. Other thoughts crept into Gawain's clearer mind.

THWONK! *I've got her. She'll do it.* CLUNK! *All I need do is not touch her. She can't stand that.*

CRASH! *Neither can I. But it's that, or my head.*

Merry's getting good.

"Good one!"

"Hah-hah! May King, guard your neck!"

Exactly what I'm doing . . .

BONK! *Honor does not forbid me to lie to her. You can lie to the devil. Besides, she's only a wild savage, like this fellow here—*

THWACK! *Who could almost make a brother knight!*

Both of them are waiting to cut my head off. Maybe this Student Druid means to do it himself.

Inner Mind cried, *Sir! Do not anger yourself! Do not—*

THUNK! *What's this?*

Gawain found sky in his eyes, then grass. A tremendous blow paralyzed his back, knocked out his breath.

God and Mary, I'm down! What comes of thinking too much.

Gawain lay flat on his back, still clutching his cudgel. While he whooped for breath, Merry jumped off his pony yelling, halloing, shaking his cudgel. "A-ho, ho-ho, woo-hoo!" Merry jigged over fallen Gawain. "Square Table beats Round!" Gawain felt the ground shake as both ponies dashed off to freedom.

He had not been bested in years. He lay in Merry's jigging shadow, looking up at the sky, sheerly astonished.

With breath and wits, anger returned. The sky in his eyes turned red. Lest Merry see Fury glare up at him and laugh louder, he closed his eyes.

Inner Mind warned, *Sir. The time has come for restraint.*

"Wowowowowow!" Merry brandished his cudgel at the sky.

Sir. Calm that anger.

Gawain found breath and struggled to sit up. His back felt broken.

"Let me, Gawain!" Merry grabbed his hand and hauled him up to sit, broken back or no. "May King, if I know the rules right, now we fight afoot. Aha!"

Fight him now, Sir, you'll kill him! Angered as you are.

Gawain muttered, "Nay."

"Nay! No? Don't you want to get even?"

Gawain ground his teeth. Quietly, then: "Our quarrel is not so serious."

"Serious? What quarrel?" Merry's dancing feet stilled.

"A joust ends now. At this point." Very gently, "You win."

Merry's feet bounded up past Gawain's aching head. "I win! I win!"

Restraint, Sir. Calm. He's only an ignorant savage.

Testing his aching neck, Gawain looked up at the sky. It was blue again, with only a thin edge of disappearing red.

Merry's feet landed again under Gawain's nose. "Let me help you up."

"No, no, no!"

"Against the rules?"

"This . . . triumphing . . ."

"That's against the rules?"

"Against custom. A knight leaves his own praises for bards to sing."

"No bards here!"

And a good thing, Gawain thought grimly.

"You can tell one, later." Gawain knelt up, then stood. Back, arms, and legs worked, reluctantly.

Merry looked disappointed. "So what do I do now?"

"Pretend there was nothing to it. You knock over a Knight of the Round Table every day."

"Ah." On the instant, Merry relaxed. All surprised joy faded from his pert jester's face. "That was exercise enough to make a man hungry. Come on, May—Gawain. Let's go see what cooks in the Men's House kettle."

"Ynis! watch what you do!" I whisper harshly. Ynis freezes where she stands, head cocked low, thin shoulders stooped. Whisper. "You've picked flowers instead of peas!"

She looks down at the plants drooping in her small fists. "Oh. Didn't mean—"

"Whisper!" No need for the neighbors to know.

Women and children harvest the pea rows, sweating under wide straw hats. Dogs play and fight up and down the rows. (Except for Granny's Brindle, who lies panting in pea-shade.) Toddlers toddle. But everyone old enough to know pea from weed works.

This work is not hard. You take a good grip on a bunch of vines and yank. Then you hurl the vines behind you onto your growing pile. Since I was Ynis-small, I've found this task strangely satisfying, fun. I like to come to the row's end and look back and see bare earth where peas used to crawl.

Granny and I work two-handed, tossing vines back over shoulder without looking around. Most neighbors work the same, to a buzz of talk and laughter. Their auras flame like fires around the field, violet, blue, green. Here and there a pink aura shows me a pregnant woman, harboring life she maybe doesn't realize yet.

Ynis dreams and dawdles in her huge white aura. She

pulls one vine at a time, in one little hand. Then she turns about and drops the vine carefully onto the pile. Or if the pile is too far, she may simply drop the vine where she stands. I dread that next-row neighbors may notice.

Why do I dread? Ynis's talents and lacks are well known. Grown up, she will be a powerful witch. If she likes, she can lounge in her hut all day and do nothing but heal, prophesy, weave spells, and brew potions.

I don't want her lonely.

The magical life is lonely enough. I want my Ynis capable in both worlds, competent with magic as with the everyday, with spirit as with body.

She murmurs, "It was the Fairy, Ma."

"Hah?"

"I went to pick his vine. He looked so sad!"

"Ah."

"So I went and picked the flowers instead."

"What about the flowers' Fairy?"

"Didn't see him."

I used to pity the Fairies too. I see them still—wee faces under-leaf, looking up—but I pay no heed. I grasp and yank and hurl anyhow.

"You don't hurt Fairies when you pick their plants, Ynis." (No more than you hurt souls when you kill their bodies.) "Just tell them, 'I need this plant for my life.' They'll understand. Your life is bigger than theirs."

"Um?"

"Truly. And if you pick fast you won't even see them. Like this. Use both hands, Ynis."

"Can't pick both hands."

"Look how far Granny's gone . . ." Brindle heaves himself out of shade now and trots slowly after her. "Sure you can pick both hands. That's why the Goddess gave you two hands."

71

"This one," Ynis flaps her little left hand at me, "this one's for magic."

"Aye. But if it never picks a pea it may wither up on you." I almost lose patience. "Come *on*! Let's catch up with Granny."

Both of Ynis's little hands seem made for magic. Very awkwardly they grasp and pull plants—most unwillingly. Yet I remember them planting these same peas with joy, pushing the wrinkled round seeds deep into raised earth. That was one task Ynis did well and quickly, and I remember her white aura tinged then with vibrant green.

And look at those loaded plants now! None so fruitful over in the neighbors' row.

Ynis's gift is for creation, not destruction. But, as Merlin sings, *Time to plant, time to pull, Time for empty, time for full* . . . Sometime, sitting in oak shade, I'll teach Ynis that song.

When? Where? Are there great shade oaks to the south?

My own hands pause on the vines. What will my Ynis do with me in the south? Here, she will always be respected. Here, she will always be loved. Should tough old Granny ever fail, eager neighbors would leap to claim little Ynis and her magical gifts. Here she would never be orphaned.

In the south . . . From what Gawain has said, I think my Ynis might not be valued there.

Hands idle on pea vines, I see her grow up as Gawain's stepdaughter. He would value her beauty (which she will have), her skills (which she will likely have none), and the chance of wedding her to some other King's Companion with whom he makes common cause.

This other King's Companion, he might be ugly, or rough. He might be a grizzled old codger. Gawain and his ilk would take little care for that.

Let me look farther, though I do not want to . . . Once wedded, my Ynis would bear child after child: sons to bear arms, daughters to wed and bear child after child, till they died of it. And I might not last to help her. In the south, Ynis could be truly orphaned.

Child after child . . . how about the children I will myself bear for Gawain? What manner of folk will they grow up to be?

Truly, all this needs thinking on.

It is my body will not let me think. "Gawain!" she cries, night and noon. "Come what may, I must have Gawain!" How cruel he is, not to touch me!

Look. Ynis's slow, unwilling hands have found a snake in the peas.

He is young and small, almost new-hatched. His slender aura wriggles, pea-green. He twists about Ynis's hands and wrists. He pauses, holds still, to look up in her face. Head cocked, she holds him up close, eye to eye. Her sparkling white aura envelops him and the plants.

I do not warn her: Ynis, a new-hatched viper has all his poison. Ynis knows that. Eye to eye with the small creature, she fills him with her self and receives his self. *Time for full!*

"Hey!" Granny calls, trudging back to us past pile after harvested pile. "What you two dreamin' for?" Her straw hat swings down her bent back. "You faintin' in the sun?" Her old feet thump earth like determined drums. "Gotta drink here, for such as faint." She hauls a skin bottle out from under her tunic, waves it at us. Brindle waves his tail high beside her.

These are my own folk. How can I leave them behind forever?

AN OWL CALLED DIRECTLY overhead.

Lady Green leaped in air. Her hand tightened on Gawain's. She stood close against him, breathing hard.

Moments later she breathed, "Real owl."

"Hah."

"Don't speak."

"You did."

"In the name of all Gods, be still!"

Full moonlight filtered down through oak leaves. Ahead, northwest, a stream gurgled. Never had Lady Green brought Gawain this way before. "Come." One careful step at a time, she led him along a barely marked trail. "Don't splash." One careful step at a time, they crossed a narrow stream.

On this side travel was suddenly easier, moonlight brighter. But tension tingled from Lady Green's hand up Gawain's arm. She was frightened.

As always, she wore her long green gown and magic girdle. Also, two dark wool cloaks. Gawain had counted on the jewelry he had seen hung in Granny's hut to pay for the journey, but he had glimpsed no glint of jewelry on her. Under the cloaks she must carry a pouch full of it. Or maybe it waited in saddlebags, on the ponies she had ready . . . somewhere. Unless she did not know the value of jewelry. That was possible. With these savages, anything was possible.

Sir, you should have mentioned it to her.

Too late now.

Crick, crunch.

She grabbed his hand tight. Whispered, "No noise, Gawain."

He lifted his foot off a white stick. No. White bone. Bone?

"Step on nothing here."

His skin prickled. Breath came strangely short. Cold dread moved up his arm from Lady Green's hand.

He was beginning to wonder if he should step on this earth here at all. But she pulled him on, over the bone, along a wider trail, past huge, ancient oak trunks. Bright silver moonlight drew his eyes upward.

"Ach!" The strangled cry gurgled in his throat. Lady Green stopped stiff in the trail.

"Hush! Gods above, what is it? Oh."

High on a trunk, a human head looked down. Green flesh dangled from bared white bone. Eye sockets met Gawain's shocked eyes.

Gawain had seen severed heads before. He had seen them in plenty, transfixed on spears, on gates, once on a savage enemy's house door. Never before had a severed head looked back at him, spoken to him. He felt this head speaking in his heart. But he could not make out the words.

Lady Green tugged urgently at his hand. "Come!"

"Who?"

"Hush!" She pulled him along.

Three more steps and he met a skull lower down, almost within reach. He started, shivered, stopped. Whispers from the past echoed in his mind. He glanced up at a forest of moon-white skulls. Those at the treetops shone brightest. Lower down hung fresher skulls, dull, flesh-ribboned—as though they were moved up, year by year, to make room, as corpses in a narrow sepulcher are moved down. God's teeth! "Lady Green!"

"Hurry—"

"Should a Christian man walk this trail?"

"What?" She stopped and turned to him, moonlit eyes

amazed at his ignorance. "No one should walk this trail. Sometimes we need to."

Whose were all these skulls? Surely they were trophies of no battle fought for life and land! The Square Table and all its ilk could hardly manage this.

"Who were all these . . . people?"

"May Kings. Come!"

May Kings. Kings of Mays stretching back to Noah and the Flood.

Sir, that's what the first head wanted to tell you. Your head would be next.

Lady Green tugged at Gawain's hand.

Dread struck a blow that set him swaying. *Gather your forces, Sir!*

Anger reddened his vision.

Now you see it! This is what yon red-haired sow planned for you. And that Student Druid. And Old Lady Granny. Satan bless them all!

He strode forward. Bones crunched underfoot. *Careful, Sir. Be not angry, here and now!*

"Hush! Slower!" Lady Green restrained him.

He whispered, "Are there guards here?" Behind oak trunks? Why should there be? The crowded skulls should be guards enough.

"Not human guards."

Horror skittered up and down his backbone, withered his innards. *Sir, we're in Satan's Dun itself!*

God and Mary, Angel Michael—

Don't, Sir. Satan might hear you. And he's closer.

Gawain followed Lady Green into a wide red clearing. Moonlight fell red on red bones, red stones, one huge flat red stone, seemingly drenched in fresh red blood.

Sir, control that anger. You need to see clear. You need to see clear!

She led him up to the great red stone and paused before it. She let his hand go. She raised both orange hands and her orange face into fading pink light. Her lips moved.

She's praying to Satan.

If I had a sword—

Sure, you'd slice off her head on the altar. And all the Demons of Hell would shriek on your trail. Whisht, now. Quiet.

Lady Green turned back to Gawain. Pale now, she reached for his hand. "Come." Carefully, she drew him through red moonlight onto a shaded trail.

GAWAIN AWOKE TO THE *whish* of morning rain on rock.

He came wide awake at once, the way he always had before he ever drank Lady Green's ale. His side ached. He turned onto his back, which ached more. He opened his eyes to a stone roof arching close over him.

He lay on a stone cave floor with Lady Green. Rain *whished* outside the cave mouth; in here they lay dry. The two cloaks she had brought almost covered them.

She had brought nothing else. No jewelry, no bag of clothes. No arms but the sheathed knife jabbed in her magic girdle. No food. "Baggage might alert suspicion," she explained last night.

Outside Satan's Dun they had found one large, brown-bristly pony tethered. "Why not two, at least, in God's name?"

"Hard enough to get one. These ponies are strong, Love. He'll carry us both." And carry them both the pony did, far and fairly fast, southward over moonlit moor.

Softly, now. Gawain sat up. Very gently he lifted his cloak aside and looked down on Lady Green. Deeply she slept, as though the cave rock were a goosedown bed. Sleeping, she smiled.

Last night they had made love. Last night he had given her all that he had withheld before.

Good thing I kept that promise, Gawain thought. *Since I won't be keeping the other. At least I gave her that.*

He had loosened her magic girdle and tossed it to the left. The green gown went right. His trousers lay crumpled at hand. Her knife fell somewhere . . . here. Gawain picked it up and tested it on his thumb. Good and sharp.

Lady Green turned toward him. Deep asleep, she drew her cloak up over freckled white shoulders. Her long red hair trailed across their grey stone bed.

God! I could strangle her with that rich red hair! That would be simple justice.

Asleep, she looked innocent and helpless.

Innocent! I saw her pray at Satan's altar last night!

Helpless! In her woman's way, this girl's as strong as I am.

Girl?

Shimmering rain-light showed slack lines in her sleeping face that he had never noticed before. *And grey hair! Holy Mary, grey hairs in the red! I think she's older than I am. Here I've caught her in another lie.*

Not a serious lie, Sir. Not like meaning to hang your head on an oak tree.

Why don't I stab her right now!

Sir, you would not stab an enemy knight, asleep.

That's true. And after all our nights together . . . nights whose like may never come again.

This is a very rare girl—woman. I almost love her.

Not surprising, Sir.

Maybe I could . . . keep my promise?

How, Sir?

Fingering her knife, Gawain brooded over the sleeping

Lady Green. *I couldn't wed this savage. She thought me ignorant. In Arthur's Dun she would seem a wide-eyed toddler!
She brings nothing. Not so much as a pouch of oatcrumbs!
Now if she'd brought all that jewelry . . . but no. Even all
that wouldn't be enough to wed.*

*No. I cannot do it. I must break my promise, though it
hurts my heart.*

*Sir. This is more than an ungallant deed you do here.
You break your solemn promise—*

A promise to a pagan savage.

*You leave a woman asleep on a wild moor, among brig-
ands, Saxons, wolves. A woman who trusts you.*

*A woman whom I trusted! She can thank her Gods I do
not stab her dead.*

Will you even take her knife, her only defense?

*I will! By the time I reach Arthur's Dun this knife will be
chipped to the handle!*

*Sir Gawain. What you are doing is unknightly. Dishon-
orable. Never till now have you stooped to dishonor.*

Never have I stood in such a case!

*Suppose Arthur learns of it? Angel Michael, Sir! Sup-
pose Merlin learns of it! Imagine the song that bards might
sing for a hundred years!*

No one will ever know.

You will always know.

*And I will always regret! More than the loss of Honor, I
will always regret the loss of my Lady Green.*

Gawain bent down and over and kissed Lady Green.
Deeply she sighed and wound both arms around his neck.
Still sleeping, she returned his kiss.

God's bones! How can I leave her!

Her arms sank away. Smiling, she resettled herself on
the stone floor.

If I had not seen Satan's Dun with my own eyes . . .

(High on a trunk, a human head looked down. Green

flesh dangled from bared white bone. Eye sockets met Gawain's shocked eyes. In his heart the head said clearly, *I am you, Sir Gawain, King's Companion.*)

God's bones! King Arthur himself would do what I do now!

Very softly he moved away, where Lady Green would not feel his movements. Stooped under the low rock roof, he drew on tunic, trousers, and boots.

Look. There beside her, her famous magic girdle. God's blood! I'll wager with that girdle she can call up a Demon to heist her home by the hair!

He worked her knife into the sash of his trousers.

Let the girdle save her now. Witness, Herod's Holy Innocents, I leave her alive. More than that I cannot do.

He did not look at her as he drew his cloak quietly off her. He did not look back at her as he ducked under the low cave lintel and stood up straight in cold, hard rain. Not far off waited the big brown-bristly pony, hobbled.

Gawain glanced around the rolling, rain-veiled moors. *Far as I can see, nothing. No one. I'll wager the Square Table fellows haven't yet noticed we've gone!*

He glanced back into cave-dimness. *If she stirs . . . if she calls now . . .* He swung the cloak over his shoulders.

Sir. Do you not go back and look at her again. Do you not.

Gawain wheeled about and strode through wet to the pony. It raised its rough head and nickered as he whipped off the hobble and reattached it as rein. He found a rock to mount from and climbed onto the pony's wet-slippery back. One last time he glanced at the low cave entrance. Nothing stirred there. Not even the pony's greeting had wakened Lady Green.

Sir. I remember you saying, "I swear to you by God, His angels and saints: when we come to Arthur's Dun we two shall be wed together." Now, for the rest of your life, you will know you have broken faith.

Gawain shrugged a mighty shrug. Rain flew from his shoulders.

Oh, come! She didn't even know the force of that vow. She's only a wild pagan, after all! In Arthur's Dun we would call her a peasant. Broken faith with her is but a small dent on my Honor.

Aye, Sir. Like a wee rust-ridge on a shining shield.

Gawain turned the pony southward, clapped heels to hide, and rode away. Swiftly the pony trotted, lightly, with but one rider.

CAROL

By no Sun's light did Mary see
Her newborn Son; our Lord was He.
Cold candle watched her new Son nurse;
That Son she brought to virgin birth,
That Sun that beams eternally,
God's Son the Christ; our Sun is He.

THE
GREEN
KNIGHT

KING ARTHUR'S YULE LOG burned high.

Horn dancers thumped about the Round Table. Their antlers cut through gathering smoke as if through morning mist. Their heels drummed like hooves. Proudly graceful, they circled the Round Table and wreathed among lesser tables.

Regally robed, gold-crowned Arthur brooded on his dais. He wore the only sword allowed in the hall besides his ceremonial sword, Caliburn, which hung, displayed, on the wall above. Like his knights, Arthur watched the Horn Dance with hooded, hungry eyes.

On her lower dais beside him, Queen Gwenevere looked over and between the dancers' horned heads to the Round Table. From under a gold circlet her red-gold braid looped down rich-embroidered breast and thigh to silken slippers. Slender hands folded and smoothed, smoothed and folded the festive gown covering her lap. Her pale gaze pierced the smoke, passed dancers and knights and Gawain, to rest on Lancelot.

Gawain felt her attention arrow past him. Hunched over his mead, he turned halfway round and saw Lancelot feel it. Lancelot looked up with bored and hungry eyes. His gaze locked with Gwenevere's. Gawain could see him forget hunger and boredom and where and when he was. King Arthur, the whole Round Table, anyone looking at Lancelot could see sorrowful love spill like tears from his eyes.

Gawain suppressed a growl.

Like all the waiting feasters, Gawain was starved. At

break of day the Round Table had attended Mass in Arthur's chapel. Next they had ridden out hunting, thirty knights with expert woodsmen, squires, oat-fed horses, and roaring hounds. After this, a break in which to bathe, comb, and change bloody, sweated clothes for festal ones. At this break, prudent men had snatched a fistful of bread, a dipper of porridge. Gawain was not a prudent man.

Now at last they came gowned, combed, jeweled, in good appetite, to Arthur's New Year feast. But they had forgotten Arthur's dreary New Year custom.

At least Gawain had forgotten—and glancing sourly about the table, he thought he was not the only one.

Not a dish was carried in, with fanfare or without. Not a crumb, not a morsel would be served until the New Year's omen appeared.

Something quite remarkable must happen now, before the eyes of the famished feasters—and Merlin must analyze, divinate, and expound upon it, and prophesy for the coming year. Only then could the feast begin.

Nursing his mead, Gawain growled louder than his stomach.

Drink was allowed before the omen. At the Round Table eyes were dimming, hands fumbling. Unless the omen appeared in the next instants, some at the table would slide under it.

Drums and dancers' feet echoed in Gawain's aching head. He glanced again at Lancelot.

Erect and attentive now, Lancelot looked steadily over Gawain's head into Gwenevere's eyes. The hunger in his face was not now for food.

A deeper growl, a comment such as the boar had made from his snowy thicket that morning, burst from Gawain. Redness crept in at the edges of his vision. Everyone

knew of Lancelot and Gwenevere. No one discussed them
aloud. But Gawain dreaded the damage this foolish affair
might do the Round Table. He saw it as a crack in the
table, which could become a split, which could widen till
the table broke in half. That could end Arthur's reign and
Arthur's hard-won Peace. And all for the love of a red-
haired bitch, Queen or no! It maddened him to see Lancelot and Gwenevere lost in admiration of each other before
the whole table, before Arthur himself.

Sir! He heard his Inner Self say. It had been saying
Sir! Sir! for some time, unable to make itself heard over
the thump of music and dance. *Sir, you must not lose control. Must. Not.*

What do you want me to do?

Maybe a drink would dampen your temper.

Nothing else to do!

Gawain seized and drained his goblet. *Women!* he
thought. The fire they lit in a man's loins could be deadlier
than enemy swords. A knight such as Lancelot should
know to guard himself against that fire. Gawain himself
had known that much.

A cool green vision floated behind his bleary eyes: his
Lady Green, as she had come to him on so many delightful
summer nights, green-robed, magic-girdled, her loose hair
moonlit fire down her breasts . . . smiling.

He shut his eyes against the next vision. But behind
closed eyes it came on brighter.

His Lady Green lay asleep on cold rock. He himself
crouched over her, testing her knife on his thumb, ready to
slice her throat on whim.

But I did not do that.

No. He left her alive. He saw himself stooped under
the cave roof, pulling on his clothes, sticking her knife in
his sash, ducking out into cold rain alone.

He saw himself ride away on the brown-bristly pony—
Nothing but a peasant knife in my sash!—and leave her
asleep, alone in a cave on a wild moor far from home.
Brigands, Saxons, and wolves roamed that moor. And she
with not even a knife . . .

*God's bones! She had her magic girdle. More than I
had.*

Gawain had not confessed that part of the story to
anyone, nor ever would. He hardly knew what to think of
it himself. What might others think?

Two small brown hands lifted a pitcher past his shoulder and refilled his goblet. These wee and slender hands
had all five fingers strangely even-lengthed. Gawain turned
to thank Niviene, Merlin's young assistant mage.

She stood like a child beside him, dark eyes intent on
the flow of mead into his goblet. Gowned in innocent
white, she might be someone's daughter, a girl too young
to appear safely even in King's Hall, with the company
hungry and drunk. But no one's daughter would wind
magic mistletoe through her coarse, dark hair. A cold wind
breathed on Gawain's heart.

Niviene's strangeness began with her small size and
even-lengthed fingers. It did not end there. She was said to
read omens and cast spells nearly as well as Mage Merlin
himself. Rumor said that those two together had cast the
evil spell that bound Lancelot and Gwenevere together;
also, that their spells maintained the borders of Arthur's
Peace. No Saxon could breathe easily within those borders. Rumor said that in the worn, patched pouch she
wore even here, even today, Niviene carried herbs to heal,
to wound, to mangle a man's mind, to kill.

Gawain had never paid much heed to such matters. He'd had better things to do and think of—until his
northern adventure last summer. A quick vision of Satan's

Dun rose in his fuddled mind and sank again. He shuddered.

Her task done, Niviene raised her eyes to his and smiled her rare, closed-mouth smile. A sharp, cold frisson ran down his spine, out arms and legs to fingertips. Barely, he managed to nod thanks.

Niviene regarded him. From the distance he had always kept between them, he had taken her for a girl. Close now, he saw faint lines in her face and ageless, cool wisdom in her eyes. To his intense relief she moved on to fill another goblet.

Suppose Mage Niviene knew what Gawain had done on the moor last summer. What would she think?

Thankfully, the din was lessening. Two by two the horn dancers careened out the great doors into the street, taking their music with them. Now only the roar of drunken talk echoed between Gawain's ears.

Take Mage Merlin himself, now. If he knew the truth, what would he think? What, in Mary's name, would he sing?

Merlin had composed a song, "Gawain, May King," based on Gawain's telling of his adventure. It began:

> *"You northern knave, what do you here?*
> *Ride your rough pony not so near!*
> *We guard King Arthur's portal, here.*
> *Stand! Or you'll maybe stop a spear.*
> *Give now your lineage and name.*
> *(If knaves have lineage and name.)*
> *That name again? Gawain?*
> *Gawain!"*

In the song, the amazed guards brought Gawain before Arthur, who recognized him with an uncle's delighted

91

embrace and commanded him to tell his adventure before the whole Round Table.

In the song, Gawain then related how he, with companions, went to spy out the north country. Saxons, brigands, and wolves killed his companions. Gawain alone escaped, starving and all but disarmed, to roam the wild moors on his white charger, Warrior.

Starving, he rode into a savage May Day celebration, expecting hospitality. He was surrounded treacherously, pulled down, captured, and crowned May King. Then he had to lie with the beautiful May Queen—half Fairy, half pagan Goddess—where he acquitted himself well, till he learned that the May King would lose his head at Summerend.

("Amazing!" listeners would murmur. But some would nod wisely and remark that they had heard such tales before.)

Recovered by then from exhaustion and hunger, Gawain caught a scruffy pony from the savages' herd and escaped, without arms or provenance, southward across the moors. On the way he killed game and brigands with his only weapon, the knife in his sash, and turned up at Arthur's gate a season later, an unrecognizable shadow of himself.

The song ended with a list of the gifts and honors Arthur showered upon his heroic nephew.

What the song did not tell—because Merlin never heard—was that the beautiful May Queen fell so deeply in love with Gawain that she helped him escape; that he broke his solemn vow to wed her, and left her alone on the moor; that he discovered only when he was safely home that he was himself in love with her.

Nor did the song tell of Gawain's nightly dreams of Lady Green: dreams of her lovemaking, of his vow-taking, and of her probable rape and death.

But she did have the magic girdle. Remember that.
If Mage Merlin knew all that . . .
God's blood! He's going to sing now!

In the relative silence after the horn dancers' departure, Merlin had taken a bench close by the royal dais. White-robed and crusted with mystic jewels, now he was tuning his harp, Enchanter. One by one, voices dropped and sank out of hearing till the hall was still.

Gawain's heart should have been beating high, hoping to hear again the glorious strains of "Gawain, May King." Rather, it shrank within; almost as if fearing to hear the true story sung.

From the corner of his eye Gawain saw Niviene pause beside the Yule fire. She had poured all her mead and left the pitcher aside. Empty-handed, she stood at the fire pit, so close her dress might have caught fire, looking across the hall at Merlin. She dipped a swift hand into her worn, patched pouch, drew something out in her fist, and tossed it into the Yule fire.

Vaguely wondering, Gawain emptied the goblet she had filled for him.

Merlin struck a commanding glissando on Enchanter's tuned strings. The last talk died away. King's Hall waited for Merlin's song, so silent that Gawain heard the Yule fire snap.

From the corner of a misty eye he saw Niviene glide away from the fire.

Merlin raised hand to harp again. Three slow, strange chords he plucked and drew breath to sing. Puzzled, Gawain felt his heart slow and hairs rise on his neck.

The wide street doors crashed open.

Merlin paused, mid-breath. Arthur stiffened on his throne.

Startled, the Round Table turned toward the doors as

one man—one strangely slow and sleepy man. Later, Gawain would feel, and hope, that from this moment the Round Table as one man fell asleep and dreamed.

Into King's Hall clattered a great green charger. In the green saddle rode a great green man. With no word, no sound but the clang of shod hooves on stone floor, he rode between the lesser tables past the Round Table, straight toward Merlin and Arthur's dais.

As best Gawain could see through newly thick smoke, the green charger was all green-furnished. The saddle was green, studded with gold and green jewels. The stirrups were green, and the bosses of the bit. The horse's green mane, well crisped and combed, was fringed with golden threads; its tail was wound in gold threads and bound about with a broad band of bright green, sewn with green stones. Golden rings jangled along the green reins.

Wreathed in smoke, the rider appeared more startling than the horse. Huge and hideous as a giant ogre, skin, hair, and bushy beard as green as the horse's hide, he rode fur-mantled and hooded. His arms were wrapped in green jeweled hoods that kings might wear. His spurs were golden, his belt covered with embroidered green silk sewn with green stones. In one green-gloved hand he carried a red-berried holly branch, in the other a huge battle-ax. The ax handle, bound about with iron bands, was wrapped in green lace. From his seat Gawain saw how sharp was the green steel blade.

Knights, pages, squires, servants—everyone in the hall held breath as this apparition clattered past them to halt before Arthur's dais.

Gawain thought, *Surely, this being is Fey!*

Everyone else seemed to hold the same thought. No one moved or spoke. Now the charger stood still. Only the crackle of the Yule fire was heard in King's Hall . . . and the continuing, slow tinkle of Merlin's harp, so soft that Gawain was not sure he heard it.

A deep, cracked roar burst from the phantom's green beard. In a strange, harsh accent he cried, "Where's the chief of this gang?" As though he were not looking crowned Arthur in the face.

No one rushed to answer. Arthur himself paused, collecting dignity like a cloak about him.

He said slowly, "I am Arthur, head of this house." *(Wisely spoke, Uncle!)* "Dismount and join us at our New Year feast. Later we can talk of your errand. I suppose you want a fight."

"Nay, nay, help me, God! I came not here to quarrel. Or I would have brought my shining bright spear, my shield and helmet and sword." The giant's booming speech hesitated while he swallowed thick spittle.

He continued, "You can see by this branch I bear that I come in peace. All men say that you are the finest King of the finest men in the world. If you are as fine as all men say, you will play the New Year game I offer you." The Green Knight turned in his saddle to look around the hall. "But I doubt it. I see here only beardless boys." No knight there, nor Arthur himself, raised voice or hand to this insult. Merlin's harp played quietly on. The Green Knight turned back to Arthur. "But, ech, it's Yule, and New Year, and you have a company here. So I offer you this game.

"If any man in this house dare give a stroke and take a stroke, I shall hand him this ax." He lifted and shook the green ax for all to note. "And I shall hold still for his stroke. Then he shall stand still for my stroke. But he shall have a year and a day to live before I strike.

"There, that's my game. Now let's see any takers."

No one spoke or moved. Merlin's harp played on, unheard.

The Green Knight turned in his saddle and reeled his red eyes around the hall. He bent his bristling green brows in a scowl and wagged his green beard in mock merriment. "Hah!" And he rhymed:

"What, can this be Arthur's house,
In many lands a story?
Where now your pride, your wrath, your rage,
Your often-vaunted glory?"

And he burst into enormous laughter.

Behind him, Merlin's harp whispered on.

Fury flushed Arthur's face deep red under his crown. He stood up and cried, "Give me that ax! By God's halo, I'll crush every bone in your body!" He cast off his ermine mantle, threw it down across Gwenevere's silken lap, and leaped down from the dais.

Surprisingly agile for his size, the Green Knight dismounted and handed Arthur his ax. While Arthur tried its swing he stroked his beard as though he'd been offered a drink, rather than death.

Gawain sat appalled, frozen in shock. As if bound in a nightmare he watched the High King risk his life in this foolhardy way because no one of his bewitched knights could move. Barely, he managed to swivel his eyes toward Lancelot.

Lancelot's hands trembled on the Round Table. He leaned a little forward, striving to break the spell that bound them all.

Gawain drew gasping breath. He, Gawain, must break the spell before Lancelot did!

A hand touched his shoulder and sent energy surging through locked muscles. Like lightning, awakeness flooded his innards. He glimpsed Niviene, just lifting her small hand away.

Gawain shot up off the bench. His locked throat opened. "Sire!" He yelled to Arthur. "Not right! Unseemly!"

Intent on hefting the great green ax, Arthur yet heard him. He looked up and gestured for Gawain to come forward.

Gawain stepped back over the bench and tried to hasten to the dais. Dizzy smoke seemed to trip him up. On his way he stumbled against several broad, seemingly paralyzed backs. The journey to the dais needed only a few strides, but Gawain arrived there panting.

Meaning to drop to one knee before Arthur, he crashed down.

"Sire." His voice cracked like the giant's. But he forced high, gallant language from his tongue. "It were unseemly that you, our High King, should risk your life on a game, while so many bold knights sit here about you."

Arthur nodded broadly to that.

Gawain continued, firmer and clearer with every elegant word. "This business is not fitting for you, nor for any of your most wise and skillful knights. All know that I am the least of your knights. My only virtue is that you are my uncle. Sire, give this game to me."

Arthur nodded to that. He could hardly refuse, for what Gawain said was simply true. He was too valuable for this foolish risk. He said, "God bless you, Nephew. May heart and hand be steady." And he handed over the green ax.

Gawain rose—more smoothly than he had knelt—and faced the giant.

"Tell me your name," the Green Knight roared. "I would know with whom I play!" His voice came hollow through the bristly green beard.

"In truth," Gawain answered with ceremonious courtesy, "I am called Gawain, I who offer you this blow, whatever may follow. And this time next year I will take your blow, with whatever weapon you choose."

"By God!" blustered the Green Knight. "You have well recited the covenant I asked of the King! Swear now by your Honor that you will seek me, a year from now, wherever you may find me, and take back the blow you give today."

"Where will I find you?" Gawain asked, testing and lifting the ax. "I know neither your name nor your country or home."

"After you have struck," the Green Knight declared, "I will tell you that. And if I cannot tell you, then you're the better off. Ha, ha! Much the better off! Come now, show me how you strike."

"Gladly, Sir, in truth."

Swiftly, for all his bulk, the Green Knight knelt down on two knees. He pushed down the neck of his fur mantle, pulled his bush of green hairs forward over his brow, and stretched out his neck.

Gawain gave himself no time to doubt or fear. Quickly he gripped the lace-wrapped ax handle and heaved the ax high. Down it dove, cut through the giant's neck as through cheese, and rang against the stone floor.

The head fell, bounced, and rolled three feet away.

Green blood fountained from the severed neck. The great green horse stepped a little aside, snorted, and defecated on the King's Hall floor.

A sigh rose from the Round Table, but no shout of triumph or relief. And a good thing this was! For the Green Knight's headless body neither slumped nor fell.

The Green Knight reached out, groping with both hands, one, two, three feet. He grasped the head by its hair and lifted it.

Then he stood up, set foot in stirrup and mounted.

With one hand he took up his reins. The other hand held out his head at arm's length toward Gawain.

The closed eyelids lifted up. The gaping mouth hardly moved, but the head said clearly, "Look you now, Gawain; you had better do as you have vowed before all the knights in this hall. Men call me the Knight of the Green Chapel. Ask for the Green Chapel, you cannot fail to find me. So come, next New Year's Day, or be called a coward forever."

With this farewell the Green Knight turned his green charger and pressed his golden spurs. The charger burst from a standstill into a canter. Its shod hooves raised sparks from stone as it thundered past the Round Table and out the wide street doors as it had entered. And all the way the Green Knight's corpse held out his open-eyed head at stiff arm's length.

Merlin's harp had been playing, unnoticed, since the Green Knight entered. Now he played a last, loud glissando, then stilled the harp strings.

King's Hall awoke slowly. Knights found they could stir a finger, uncurl a lip. They drew breath and looked at each other.

King Arthur and Gawain stood stiffly together by the dais. Gawain leaned on his new battle-ax, which dripped slow, green slime on the floor.

With waking eyes, Gawain saw a holly branch in berry near his feet and, five feet away, a pile of steaming horse shit.

Arthur cleared his throat. "Well done, Nephew!" He laid an arm about Gawain's shoulders. "Let your ax hang up here by Caliburn, where all can see it and admire your courage." He gestured to a dazed servant to take and hang the ax.

He turned to Gwenevere, who sat like a white wooden

statue, his shed mantle across her knees. His voice rose and took on assurance. "Dear Lady, look you not so dismayed! This is Yule time! Good it is at Yule to laugh, to sing carols, to act out plays." Gwenevere managed a weak smile.

Arthur turned to the Round Table. "Now have we all seen a marvel, and an omen for the New Year. Let Mage Merlin interpret the omen."

Merlin stood, stroked his beard, and thought. After a long moment he said, "Gawain has cut off the head of Enmity. Arthur's Peace is well established. Yet danger may arise. Next New Year's Day may find the Peace again at risk. Vigilance is ever called for."

Arthur clapped loudly. He pulled a gold ring from his hand and went across to Merlin to deliver it himself. "And now, Round Table, let us feast."

Horns blew. Doors opened; the feast marched in. Huge dish after fancy dish was paraded before the dais, then placed out on the Round Table and lesser tables. Boar heads biting apples, stuffed cockatrice, swans re-dressed in shining feathers, all manner of breads and cakes filed past Gawain, famished only minutes ago; yet now, wreathed in delicious aromas, with little desire to indulge. Arthur murmured, "Go, Nephew. Feast. Show them a bold, hearty appetite!"

Arthur mounted the dais, took back his mantle from the pale Queen and sat down. Dazed, Gawain returned to his seat at the Round Table. A boar's head sat on a pile of ham before him. Someone had already snatched the apple from its gaping jaws.

He reached for the ham, but the boar's dead gaze woke words in his mind. *Look you, Gawain, you had better come to the Green Chapel next New Year's Day. Or be called coward forever.*

The boar's dead eyes reminded him of moonlit heads nailed to oak trees in Satan's Dun.

Hungry—starving—Gawain drew back his hand from the dish.

MIDSUMMER SONG

I am the Green Man
Who is the Tree
That shades and shelters
Mortality.

THE
GREEN
MAN

ONE COLD, DARK NOON last cold, dark winter, Ynis remarked, "Ma. Your cloud's rosy."

We sat in here where I sit now, remembering, under the smoke hole. Rather sadly, we choked down our last Brindle soup, old Brindle's last gift to us. (If Granny had not bonked him in his sleep, someone else would have. Dogs were already scarce in hungry Holy Oak.)

Ynis squinted at me through smoke and said, "Your cloud's rosy."

Granny gave her a small, grim nod. "Your Ma's got a Little in there."

"In her stomach?"

"Where Littles grow."

They talked on together, between themselves; not to me.

Ynis cocked head, widened eyes. "It's got its own cloud!"

GRANNY: Aye. It's got its own self.

YNIS: Don't look like a Little! Looks like a . . . fish.

GRANNY: Got a heap of growin' to do. When it's born it'll look human.

YNIS: What's it eat?

GRANNY: What your Ma eats.

YNIS (Thoughtful): Oh-oh.

GRANNY (Nodding): Aye.

YNIS: Does it have a dad?

GRANNY: Most times Littles do.

YNIS: Is it a he or a she?

GRANNY: You tell us.

Ynis came scrambling around the dead fire to me. Kneeling beside me, she placed both small hands on my stomach, then laid her ear there. Long she listened to Brindle soup gurgle within, to innards grind and air groan, to the flops and flips of the "fish" that I could not yet feel.

She lifted a disappointed face. "It's a he."

Disappointment chilled my bones, too.

Granny shrugged. "Goddess dreams up boys, too."

For the first time Ynis's dark, widened eyes met mine. "Ma. Do you want a boy Little from that bad dad?"

I folded thinning hands over my belly. I said, "Ynis. This is my Little, given me new and fresh from the Goddess Herself. And he need not answer for his dad. He need answer only for himself, and that only after he is grown."

Across the dead fire, Granny nodded.

From that day she gave most of her dwindling food portions to Ynis, and to me, and to Dace within me.

Therefore Granny lies here now dying.

Midsummer morning sunlight slants through our thatch. I catch myself thinking that I must rethatch. Such foolish thoughts mist into my mind, hoping to hide or soften this moment's truth.

Sunlight dapples Granny's pillow. It has not yet reached her sunken, wasted face. I think she may be gone before it does.

Drums sound from Fair-Field. The Tribe has been gathering all night for Midsummer. My jeweled green gown hangs ready, behind me. Soon as Granny goes I must rise quickly, dress, and bring the Goddess out to Fair-Field.

Should I fail, an eager substitute waits, a student druidess from Camp-Field Village. There creeps in another misty thought, to ease this dreadful moment!

For this moment, which should be solemn, is dreadful. Granny is going away. I am losing my Granny. Even now I am almost alone.

Not truly alone. Ynis sits cross-legged on Granny's other side, dressed, like me, in her oldest rags. (Later, we will throw these rags away.) She waits and watches coolly, as I should, armed in ceremonial calm.

In his basket beside me, newborn Dace stretches soft, unswaddled legs and sighs.

No, I am not alone. But after this I shall be chief of our family. I shall stand alone between heaven and earth, Gods and men, and these children, even as I stand now between heaven and our Tribe.

Granny gasps. Ynis leans forward, interested. "Ma," she whispers, "look at her cloud."

Granny's grey aura fades and shrinks with every gasp. I groan. Granny slits filming eyes to look at me. I mutter, "My fault!"

Granny should dispute this. She should comfort me. I think she can still speak. Or she could wag a finger. She only watches me with her fading squint.

I moan. "A fair harvest last fall, and you would be dressing now for Midsummer!"

Yet this was not all my fault. It was his fault! It was the Gods' fault! Did I not lead him before Their very altar, show him to Them, show Them what I meant to do? They could have stopped us! Then, we were already past the guards. But the Gods could have sent an omen. The Green Man could have swung out of the oaks and torn us to shreds. The Gods were silent. They let me lead him away south. Only then, only after that, came the relentless rains that rotted the grain and the fall peas.

It was his fault! To save his precious life and blood he ran away. He left the Tribe to starve. Anger tightens my breath till I gasp.

"Gwyn . . ."

I startle. "Granny?"

"Don't . . . call . . . Spirit here."

109

"Spirit?"

"Evil. When you think of him . . . Spirit comes . . . storm cloud. Not now, Gwyn."

"Oh. I think I know . . ." That spirit. My nameless Demon.

"You know! Can't see . . . can feel."

Aye. I feel it now, settling over my head like last summer's clouds.

"Every time you think . . . Gawain . . ."

"Gawain!" I spit the name out like poison.

"Spirit comes. Eats anger. Steals power."

I lean closer, shading Granny's pillow from creeping sunshine. "Granny! It promises me more power!"

"Lies. That one gives little. Takes all." Granny gapes and rattles. "It'll harvest you, Gwyn. You'll be . . . an empty pod . . . when it is through. Took me years to . . . be me again."

That's right. Granny knows. "How do I fend it off? What should I do?"

"Think . . . good."

Think good. This moment, this hut is my world. And there is nothing good in this world to think of.

Granny whispers, "Think . . . Goddess. You will be Goddess soon."

Aye, out in Fair-Field in full Midsummer sun. Now, that hardly seems real.

"Think . . . Ynis."

I glance across Granny at Ynis. Calmly she returns my gaze.

My child sits erect in rough rags, her braid newly neat down her slender back, her soft, lovely face thoughtful as a matron's.

"Ynis will bring joy . . ." Aye. She will. Already she has brought joy.

"Think . . . Dace."

110

I look down at Dace in his basket. He wiggles, kicks, squirms, and screws up his sleeping face to cry.

Most newborns lie swaddled, bound to a board. Folk say they feel safer like that, warm and confined, as in the womb. And they are certainly quieter than my babes. Granny would not let me swaddle mine. "Binds up their spirit," she said, when Ynis was born. "Keeps 'em always a bit sleepy, all their life. Like they can't stretch out just all the way."

Now Dace opens his wee pink mouth and cries. I gather him up, with all his squirms and wiggles. I open my rags and set him to my breast. The pink mouth grabs and pulls. Sweetness flows through me, around me.

"There," Granny murmurs, "it's going now."

I feel it going, the dark cloud moving away, disappointed. But I tell Granny, "It can't go far. It lives in me."

"Sure," Granny gasps. "Sure it does. Whole world lives . . . in you. . . . Listen."

I stoop down over Dace to hear the next faint, slow words.

"Wed. Father for babes."

Ynis leans down and says, "Merry is my Da, Granny."

"Wed . . . Merry. Guide . . . Tribe . . . together. Old One . . . old Druid . . . he will not last long . . ."

I remember a forgotten message. "Granny! He came to bless you. You were asleep."

"Think I didn't see? Saw . . . Death Wings . . . on his shoulders! Can't last long."

"Granny, does the sun bother you?" Creeping, thatch-dappled sunshine has reached Granny's face. She squints, turns her head away.

"See you! Children, sit me up. Up!"

Granny grasps Ynis's hand. With a vast effort she pulls herself upright and reaches out for my hand. I settle Dace across my knees, my breast still in his mouth, and take her hand. Cold! Out of the sunlight her eyes open wide and take in my face. "There . . . I can breathe . . ." For moments. Granny's aura has misted from her body entirely. The last of it wreathes her white hair, ready to float away.

"You and Merry . . . rule Tribe for good of all."

"Be sure of that."

"Or won't rule long. Keep Secret."

"Oh, yes!"

"She forgives you. Forgive self." (The unforgiving Goddess forgives? For the first time ever, Granny must be mistaken. She mistakes her own kind and mortal heart for that of the Goddess.)

"Beware . . . Demon. Don't . . . let it harvest you."

The hut door unlatches itself and swings open. Sunlight floods in, along with brighter light.

"That one . . . May King . . . forget. Think children. Tribe. Gods. Ah."

Granny's filmed eyes turn from my face to the doorway. "You!" I see there only sunlight, and brighter light. "Knew you'd come!" To me, Granny breathes, "You live for me." She sinks back on the sun-speckled pillow. Her breath rattles harshly. We watch the last of her aura drift away through the open door.

Moments later, or a long time later, the rattle stops.

Dace has been squirming, complaining of my breast in his face. I sit up straight and let go Granny's stony hand.

Ynis lets go the hand she holds. She stands up, shakes herself, and stretches. That's one task finished.

I ask her, "Who came? Who took Granny away?"

"Dunno, Ma. Just light."

"I saw light, too."

Sternly, little Ynis tells me, "You gotta dress, now."

"Aye." But I do not move, except to lift Dace to my shoulder and burp him.

"You gotta get out there."

The Fair-Field drums sound louder. *Come!* they call. *Hurry!* If I do not go soon, the student druidess from Camp-Field will be the Goddess.

But I can't move. It is as though my soul has gone away with Granny into light, and all that sits here is . . . as Granny said, an empty pod.

"Ma!"

"I can't move."

Ynis cocks head, plants small fists on hips. "You gotta move. Now." Her aura shoots up around her, high as the thatch—maybe beyond the thatch. It fills the whole hut with silver light.

(When Ynis was born I marveled at her huge aura. But Granny said calmly, "Sure, a Little's aura can be stronger than a druid's. Maybe she was a druid, last time.")

Now I see it expanded as never before. I hold Dace off from my shoulder and see his new, vague eyes wide open, eager, drinking in this light.

Ynis comes carefully around to me, holding up her ragged tunic so as not to touch the corpse. She stands behind me and sets her two little hands on my two shoulders.

Energy flows down through me such as I have not felt in years: the over-spilling energy of childhood, joined with awesome, druidic energy. If my body were the world, it would have swung in this moment from Midwinter to Midsummer.

Satisfaction oils Ynis's harsh young voice. "Now you can move!"

"Ech, aye!" Yet I hold the dead hand a little longer; I pat it, kiss it, let go slowly.

"Ma!"

"You take Dacie."

Ynis swoops, catches Dace from my shoulder, and plunks him against her own bony shoulder. He wails. But I need not tell her to hold his wobbling head steady. She's already a practiced hand.

"Now, Ma."

"Aye." I look my last on Granny's dead face. This worn, starved face was the Goddess's face for me, for the Tribe. Now, the Goddess's face must be my own.

I rise up. I take the largest of our stacked mats and lay it over the corpse.

Ynis says, "I'll help you dress."

"Aye." I take command. "You'll help, for sure. Run Dace over to Aesa's hut, she can take care of him. Then throw a cloak over those rags, and run out to Fair-Field. Tell the head drummer I come, and he must drum without pause till I come. This will give Granny time to pass from our midst."

"Aye, Ma!" Ynis looks a little taken aback, but relieved to see me take charge.

"Then run back here and change your dress." I lift it down from the ridgepole for her. "Put it on front in front, back in back, all by yourself. And don't get soot on it! Remember all of this. All of this matters."

"Of course I'll remember."

"You are a good girl, Ynis. At this time you need to be especially good."

"I know that."

"And say nothing, at the Field, about . . . Granny. No talk of Death at the feast of Life."

"I know that."

I hear myself say in Granny's own voice, "Sure you know!"

Alone with the corpse, I latch the door and take off my rags: my work clothes of many years, too wretched to hoe or harvest in, and now stained and smirched with death. After the festival I will burn them.

Out in Fair-Field, the shrill of pipes joins the drums.

Granny had a treasure she kept hidden in the chest behind everything else: a mirror, old and foreign, a relic of some long-ago raid or trade. She used it for magic. Now, so shall I.

I bring it out and hang it from the roof, as she used to do. Naked, I stand before it.

I stand there before myself: tall, large-boned, thin. All through the past, thin year Gawain cost us, Granny gave her food to us, to Ynis and Dace and me. Now Ynis and Dace are perfect, Granny is dead, and I am thin. When Dace was born I was amazed to find myself so light! I was never thin before, and I have not yet learned thinness. I do not yet feel like my real self.

The mirror shows me skin sagging over bones, and full breasts, thank the Goddess! Hair rich and red as ever, all that seems left of my old self; sad, angry grey eyes; and a grey aura.

Those eyes, that aura, must change. Now.

I am about to put on my ceremonial green gown, green crown and jewels. I am about to take up my barley sheaf and walk out onto Fair-Field as the Goddess embodied.

The Goddess may never forgive; but never is She angry or sad. She will not enter a sad, angry body with a grey aura, no matter how many holy verses and prayers I repeat.

And I have not much time.

I step close to the scarred, dented mirror, look close into my own eyes. Granny said, *Forget.* But before I forget, I need to remember. Remembrance is the door to Forgetting.

THE RATTLE OF RAIN on rock woke me.

Eyes yet closed, I felt rough rock under me. Shaking with chill, I wondered why I lay asleep on rock, with no blanket?

Then I remembered.

I thought, *I lie in a moor cave with my love, my pearl of price. For his sake I have given all that I had, and now I have only him.* I remembered our loving of the night before. *And just now he kissed me!* I smiled to remember that kiss.

I reached out a hand to touch him, wake him. We must be off, or the questing Square Table might yet find us.

My hand found him not.

I reached farther. As far as I could reach, I touched only cold rock. My eyes opened. Rock floor rose to meet rock ceiling. Gawain and his cloak were gone.

I said, "Love?" No answer. I felt myself alone.

Ech. He's gone outside to piss.

Feeling like that myself, I sat up and looked for my dress. It lay bunched beside me, with the magic girdle. My knife was likely under the pile.

Thankfully I pulled on the dress, tied on the girdle, looked for my knife.

No knife.

Well, that knife was the only weapon/tool we had between us. Gawain must have taken it outside.

I got up and pulled on the cloak that had lain over me, scant protection from the night chill. I drew on my sandals. (I had not dared wear boots out to my bower last night. Someone would have noticed, for sure. Someone would have whispered, "Does Gwyneth go a-journey now, at night?") Stooping under the cave roof, I went to the entrance. Rain fell, a cold curtain across the landscape. I peered out to where we had left the hobbled pony.

No pony.

So, he had hobbled away. He must have left hoofprints in the wet. We could trail him.

I looked for Gawain to loom up out of the rain, coming home to the cave. No Gawain.

Maybe . . . maybe the Square Table had found us. Killed Gawain. Taken the pony back home. Left me here for outlaws and Saxons to find.

I sneaked out into the rain, plastered myself against the cave wall, studied the moor. Birds called through rain. Crickets chirped. Unless there was someone on the hill above and behind the cave, no human life was to be found here. But the rain-drenched grass at my feet held Gawain's bootprints, clear as in snow.

My pearl of price had walked from where I stood, not long ago. One pair of prints led away. None returned.

I followed the prints. Out from the cave I paused to look up at the hill above. Nothing. No one moved there. Hungry, hurting from our rock bed, I followed my love's track to where it met the pony's track. Here I found cropped grass and hoof marks, circling about; dung; and the end of Gawain's track.

No bootprint pressed grass beyond this point. But hoof marks led away directly south, a little heavier, deeper printed, moving faster than the pony would have by his own will.

Like an erect stone, like a chief's grave marker, I stood unmoving in heavy rain.

Ach! My Demon cleared his throat in mine. His rusty voice croaked, *Told you he wouldna' wed.*

Rage came into my feet first, as if from the cold ground. Rage rose up my legs, through belly to heart. Rage lodged there, with the Demon.

117

Foolishly, I had loved Gawain. More foolishly, I had trusted him. For Gawain I had sacrificed my Tribe, my Granny—even my Ynis!

Richly had I deserved this common fate, told in so many stories, sung at so many lonely hearths! And this agony, stabbing up from the Goddess's earth, was only a beginning of agonies—a foretaste of divine revenge.

Let me out of this! I clapped hand to the knife in my girdle. No knife. Gawain had taken my life, my heart, my only weapon. I cried into the rain, "Never love again! Never again!"

Had I not loved I would be waking this morning in my bower, Gawain's head on my breast, sentry owls hooting protectively in rainy shadows. I would be my Tribe's darling May Queen, their next ruling witch. All that I had given up, as the foolish trader gave up all his jewels for one pearl.

If the Tribe takes me back after this, I will be the most faithful, most loyal witch they ever had.

Hah! The Tribe will nail your *head to a sacred oak instead of Gawain's!*

I despaired. *Let that be as the Gods will.*

That decided, immediate problems made themselves felt. Grief and rage could no longer mask my hunger, dripping cold, and danger. What should I do?

I could wait in the cave till the Square Table found me. That could be a long wait, alone with my Demon, with death at the end.

South and north were not the only directions. I could walk west or east. Huge, the wet world spread itself before me.

Lawless men, by far more dangerous than wolves, haunted the moors. We knew something of them, and Gawain had told me more. And if I came through their midst to a strange village, of a strange tribe, there I would be a slave.

Let it be as the Gods willed. I turned north.

Home would be a long, long walk in soggy clothes, on an empty stomach. If only I could graze on thick wet grass and clover, like a pony!

I slouched up the cave hill. Rain slowed around me, and stopped, and I saw north ahead: rolling, flowery moor; rolling, rising mist.

Gawain had ridden these empty moors for days before he found our May Day feast. Now I knew how hungry, how desperate he was, that he had charged in among us without a cautious thought! He might have pulled his white Warrior away, back into the oak grove he knew not enough to fear. We would never have known.

Now I, too, charged to my death, one drenched step at a time.

Through banking mists, one white cloud advanced slowly toward me. I stopped, stretched, strained eyes to see. Was it the Square Table?

Nay. Not a mob of men and ponies; it was one being . . . a God? Nearer it moved . . . a giant white horse, like a giant white cloud.

Only one horse like that drew breath in our world: Gawain's Warrior. He must have escaped unseen, even as Gawain and I escaped. But he was not wandering, grazing step by step. He was making straight toward me, at a steady walk.

Nearer he came, and I saw his rider. He saw me at the same moment, and waved.

Jaunty, cheerful, he rode up beside me and stretched down a hand. His wide green and violet aura shone steadily. Instantly, without a doubtful thought, I grasped his hand and struggled up Warrior's summer-fattened side to perch behind him. Gratefully, I hugged his waist and

leaned my wet cheek against his wet shoulder. He used the
rein in a graceful, Gawain-taught gesture, and Warrior circled himself about and headed north.

"Who sent you, Merry?"

Over his shoulder: "Me. I sent me."

Maybe . . . just maybe . . . the Square Table hadn't
yet noticed? "Are you the only one who . . ."

"Knows he ran out? Nah! Fellows runnin' like grouse
around the village! Women shakin' out blankets in case
he's inside 'em. Turnin' over iron kettles he could hide in. I
left while the Square Table was catchin' ponies to come
after." Laughter lurked in his dear voice.

"What about . . ."

"What about what?" Warrior paced steadily north
toward a faint, new rainbow.

"Me. What about me, Merry?"

"You? They're all in a mighty uproar rage about you,
Gwyn."

My arms tightened on his waist. I murmured into his
dark hair, "The Gods willed it so."

"Aye, the Gods must have willed it, or it wouldn't have
happened. Right?"

"Ah . . . aye. What I mean."

"They could have stopped him dragging you off for a
hostage, with nothing more than the clothes on you."

I heaved a great sigh into his ear.

"Ech! Such bold disrespect for a May Queen, let alone
a witch! Downright sacrilege. They're all poppin' an' hissin'
like coals back there."

I squeezed his waist, drew myself into his back.

Ech! My Demon cleared its throat. It sounded surprised, and not pleased—but ready to take advantage. *Ech.
You can yet get him back for us.*

I would if I could!

We got plan.

Riding in tired silence, I let Demon anger fill me, as a worm fills a pod. After-while I murmured, "Merry, I'll get him!"

"How you goin' to do that? He's well gone."

"For now. He's gone for now. But I can get him back."

"Ah! You have a plan?"

"I'm making one now." We rode on for a bit. Then, "I'll nail his head to an oak, Merry. You'll see me do it. But first, I'll break him."

"Hah?"

"First I'll break his pride."

"Hah!"

"Aye, that stubborn pride he wears like armor. I'll lay his armor in pieces on the ground!"

"You and me, Gwyn." Merry said this over his shoulder seriously, with no hint of laughter.

"You! You'll help me?"

"Anyhow I can."

"Oh! Ooooh!" I hugged him savagely, exultantly.

"But I tell you something first."

"Tell!"

"You want to watch that Demon."

My arms froze at his waist. "Demon . . ."

"Aye," he said, still serious. "I can see it."

More than I could do! "What does it look like, Merry?"

"Ungood, Gwyn. Not a handsome fellow."

I felt the Demon's angry response within.

"Right now, I feel it. Like fire at my back."

"It will help us catch him."

"Right enough. But don't let it take you over. Own you." Never had I heard Merry so serious!

"I'm strong, Merry."

"I won't love a Demon, understand. Won't wed a Demon."

"Once we get him back . . . break his pride . . . nail

his head . . . we'll be rid of the Demon." An angrier response still.

"So may it be," Merry said prayerfully.

Slowly we rode on toward the brightening rainbow.

THAT NAKED, SCRAWNY WOMAN in the mirror—she with the grey skin, grey eyes, grey aura—she is I.

I who was whole and hearty, quick to laugh; maybe not beautiful, but love-skilled; I who *felt* beautiful, and good, and one with the Goddess; I have come to this. Gawain brought me to this.

And not only me! My Tribe, which was strong and numerous, is now reduced. Most families around us have suffered as mine has. Granny's death, probably the last death Gawain will bring about, is far from the only one!

Gawain moves behind my eyes, dark and lithe and proud. Proud!

What is he like now? Has he changed as I have? Is my revenge working on him?

We catch him!

In the mirror, my eyes open wide. Stop! Wait!

We give you healing, Gwyn. Prophecy.

Not now. Go away. The Goddess comes.

You be greater witch than Granny, Gwyn.

The Goddess comes.

Not with us here!

Go! Go! I turn you away. I reject you.

Ha-hey-ho!

Listen, Demon. Hear those drums? Those pipes?

You think we fear music?

Aye. You fear this Midsummer music.

The drums thump, *Come!*

I will go out there green-clad, flower-crowned, bearing my sheaf of young barley. Not I, but the Goddess in me, will go out to my eager, hopeful Tribe that waits for Her. I can take no evil spirit with me.

Eh! Try to get rid of us!

She will.

I say aloud:

> *"Come to us, Lady, Sun's bright bride,*
> *Come from moor and mountainside.*
> *Come from water, come from air,*
> *Come, with us Your life to share."*

I stretch to lift my green gown down from the roof. In Granny's blotched mirror I watch it float down over my sad, sagging body. The gown hides my poverty, as winter snow hides the Goddess's brown earth. My hair glows red. A hint of color creeps into my cheeks.

> *"Stay with us, Lady; grow the green grain!*
> *Radiate sunshine, radiate rain."*

I take down my necklaces, bracelets, rings—all the sacred jewels Gawain thought I should have taken away that night. Now I understand why. If I had brought my jewels, would he have left me?

Why not? He took knife. Would take jewels.

No! No! *Get away!*

> *"Come to us, Lady, Sun's bright bride!*
> *Stay with us, Lady, in us abide."*

Slowly I fasten the emerald necklace, push the jade bracelets up my thin arms. They clank and fall off.

I could string them on a thong, use them as another necklace.

The drums thump, *Come!*

No time. Forget the bracelets. Forget the rings, which also fall off. Maybe after all, this is fitting, this bare severity, after the year we have had.

From the Demon, utter silence.

Quickly now, I redden lips and cheeks, darken brows.

"Come to me, Lady, live You in me.
Shine You in me, that mortals may see."

Now at last, the magic girdle. I have not worn it since . . . Don't think about that.

I take it down. It shines in my hands with its own green, gold-shot aura.

I wind it twice around me! And tie it. In the mirror I watch green and gold glow through my grey aura. As when you touch a rush-light to fire, and the tip flares . . . Light enters me. Fills me.

Fills whom? No one. There is no one here but Light.

Light crowns Herself with Her own flowers and takes up Her barley sheaf.

The drums thump, *Come! Come! Come!*

A walking golden torch, Light glides from the sad, dim hut toward Fair-Field.

LATE IN THE MORNING, smoke still drifts up from the Midsummer Fire ashes.

Under tents and awnings all over Fair-Field, folk lie dead asleep. A woman carries water from the stream; another brings Midsummer coals to light a breakfast fire. A few children run the field with fewer, yipping dogs. Children and dogs are blessed famine survivors.

From the village, bearers carry a covered corpse on a bier. They avoid Fair-Field. Even now, festivities over, they lug their burden the long way around toward the distant Green Chapel, home of the dead.

Later I will deal with them, and with their burden.

Right now I sit just within the fringe of oak grove, across the stream from Fair-Field and a little above, with sleeping Dace in his basket, Merry, Merlin, and Merlin's daughter Niviene.

I knew her for his daughter the moment I saw her small, dark face with his brows, and especially her fingers, even-lengthed like his. They lie idle, laced in her lap, while Merlin's fingers stray restlessly over the strings of his harp, Enchanter.

Merlin did not introduce Niviene as his daughter, but as his "assistant mage." They do not refer to their obvious relationship; so Merry and I do not either.

I have heard rumors of Niviene. She is almost as famous as Gawain's witch mother, Morgause. Rumor says truly that she is the size of a twelve-year-old boy and dresses like one. Rumor exalts her powers but does not add that her violet aura has nearly the breadth of Merlin's white one.

Warm and pink, Dace sleeps in his basket beside me. Merry sits easily against an oak and watches the rest of us with tired, smiling eyes. Bright on his breast glints the silver medallion—I gave him it last Midwinter—engraved with a Green Man's head swallowing—or vomiting?—leafy vines.

As Merlin's music ripples, his aura shimmers, sunshot. Enchanter itself seems to shine with its own, eerie aura. Merlin remarks, "The whole ceremony was right.

Very effective, despite difficulties. The joust was a new touch!"

"New as the Square Table." Merry nods.

"I noticed stirrups on the ponies. You must have learned that on your journey."

Merry says nothing.

"Too bad the wheel broke."

Enchanter whispers. Merry and I are silent.

Merlin adds, "But that made for excitement! And it's not necessarily a bad omen, taken together with all the rest. The Green Men were most impressive!"

Merry's habitual smile lurks.

"Especially the Dancing Trees."

Merry cocks his head and grins.

"And look at your fields!" Merlin nods eastward at the oat, pea, and millet fields. "Knee-high already."

"Aye." Merry spits briefly to the side. "They were knee-high last year too. Now we cannot even offer you ale."

"Have no fear." Merlin strums more strongly. "Stars, birds, and standing stones predict a good harvest. And you have a good May pair. Who's the girl?"

"Alva, from Spring-Field."

"Fine, handsome King."

Merry nods. "Willing."

"Volunteer."

"Right."

"The best kind. Did you hear my new ballad about one of King Arthur's Companions, who was once a May King?"

I startle. My eyes, which had been drifting closed, spring open. Merry snarls quietly. "How can a man have once been a May King?"

"This one was unwilling. Not a volunteer. He escaped." Modestly offhand, Merlin adds, "The whole south now sings my ballad. I call it 'Gawain, May King.'"

Merlin sits straighter, plants Enchanter more firmly on his knee, and sings.

> *"You northern knave, what do you here?*
> *Ride your rough pony not so near!"*

("Remember, this is a southern song.")

> *"We guard King Arthur's portal, here.*
> *Stand! Or you'll maybe stop a spear . . .*
> *That name again? Gawain?*
> *Gawain!"*

At the hated name, anger stirs like sickness in my deep belly. No longer smiling, Merry's eyes meet mine. *Easy, now. Give nothing away!* For the rest of the song Merry looks east, I look west.

The song is long and insulting. (Merlin trusts us to understand bias, even against ourselves.) Untruly, it tells of Gawain's escape by his own cunning and courage, and the trials and dangers of his journey home on a "rough pony" with only the knife in his sash. Looking away, I can hear Merry's teeth grind. Fury churns my stomach.

At last the wretched song ends.

> *"Now bring the bowl about again!*
> *Drink to the deeds of dread Gawain!"*

That repeated name, repeated again, sickens me.

Merlin slaps a last resounding chord from Enchanter and beams at Merry and me. "But then, his escape brought a new, weird doom upon him."

Merry sits up away from his tree. "Hah?"

"I call this song, 'The Green Knight.'"

"By all Gods, Druid Merlin, sing it!"
"This way it goes. . . . Ahem."

> *"To Arthur's Dun on New Year's Day*
> *Came noble knights with ladies gay*
> *To feast and fun, to sing and play . . ."*

The Round Table sat down to feast. But Arthur would not let one bite be bit, until a New Year's omen should appear.

Abruptly, Enchanter whangs and thumps. Dace in his basket throws out startled, tiny arms and scowls.

> *"Into the hall there charged a charger,*
> *Greener, grimmer, loftier, larger . . ."*

Merry leans forward, silent laughter loud in his face. His aura spreads and shimmers, entranced.

Niviene meets my eye and smiles her closed-mouth smile.

> *"This ogre, green ax hefted high,*
> *And his green charger, prancing nigh,*
> *They must be Fey! But such have never*
> *Darkened the door of King's Hall, ever!*
> *Never would dare those pagan sprites*
> *To breach this hall of Christian knights."*

Knowing pours into my mind, like spring water into a pool. Niviene's careful closed-mouth smile hides sharp-filed incisor teeth.

Small, dark Niviene is of the fearsome Fey. She comes here to us from the depths of an enchanted forest, from which no adventurer returns.

Ech, well. No such great surprise. After all, Druid Mer-

lin himself is said to be a Demon's child. How many hold
that against him?

Not all of us choose our parents wisely.

> " 'Come to my chapel, or coward be.
> Knight of the Green Chapel, all men know me.
> Seek me and find me, my chapel at morn.
> Your head will my chapel fitly adorn.'
> Gawain leaned on his ax, with Fey blood all green.
> No grief or fear in his face to be seen,
> No fear or grief in his heart to be found,
> Gawain, the best knight that ever trod ground."

Niviene tilts her head. Her eyes squint, then widen. I'll
wager she is studying my aura. With an effort I pull it in
close, damp down any flaming color it may show.

With a final triumphant twang, Enchanter falls silent.
Merlin twinkles at Merry. "You're sure you've got no ale
buried like gold?"

Merry grunts as his awakened aura collapses in
around him. "Water." He feels for the water bottle behind
him, hands it across.

Merlin drinks deep. "Hah! Singing is thirsty work." He
wipes his beard on his richly embroidered sleeve. "Let me
tell you, the knight is wonderfully brave under this doom.
He eats, drinks, and jousts. In truth, he does not laugh.
And his famous temper is a trifle edgy."

Merry proclaims through his teeth, "No more than he
deserves! Famine must have followed his cowardly escape."

"True. That Tribe is thinner than before. But it sur-
vives. Even some of its herds survive! Indeed, led by an
unknown chief, Demon or God, that Tribe is training an
army!"

129

"Most likely to ward off the Saxons. They are becoming seasonal pests."

Merlin agrees. "Most likely the army is for the Tribe's own defense. But its intent agrees well with King Arthur's intent."

Merry shrugs. "Lynx and cat seize the same prey."

Niviene speaks softly, abruptly, to me. I am a trifle slow to follow her strangely accented words. A moment I stare into her wide, perceiving eyes. Then the words catch up with me. "Gwyneth. I suppose you know that a Demon haunts you." She sees the Demon in my aura. Merry once said he saw it.

"My grandmother said—"

I bite my tongue. Even now, Midsummer second morning, I will not mention death, or the dead.

A voice in the deep back of my mind whispers, *Get that May King back for us, Gwyn. We make you more powerful than Niviene.*

That would be Power, indeed.

Gently, Merlin asks, "Your grandmother saw this Demon?" He squints at me, and shudders, seeing it himself. Both Merlin and Niviene expand their sparkling auras to guard against my Demon.

"Aye," I mumble uneasily. "Gran—she warned me against it."

Niviene says, "She was right to warn you. That Demon could take you over entirely, Gwyn. Own your soul. Your anger invites it."

"That's what . . . she said."

"Do not feed it on anger. Once in its power, you could never be the Goddess again. You would be good only to blast unborn babes and crops, to call in plague and nail heads on oaks."

"It . . . it promises me power."

"Power to use for its purpose. Not yours." Niviene sits

straight and still, even-lengthed fingers laced in lap. She has hardly moved since we sat down here. Only her violet aura shifts and shines, warding away my Demon.

Certainly, Niviene is powered by no Demon! Goddess Light gleams about her.

Merlin whangs Enchanter's strings again. His hands seem as restless as Niviene's are nerveless. "Gwyneth, I wish you could see Gawain, King's Companion, when he thinks himself unseen! Then he turns so dark and dour, merriment would drive that Demon straight out of your heart."

Merry laughs. Niviene and I smile. But I know well that Gawain's dour-dark misery would only whet my Demon's appetite.

Niviene remarks in her Outland accent, "You have a beautiful daughter."

We turn and follow her gaze.

Whiteness gleams among oak trunks, shines in shadow. From the deep grove walks Ynis, erect and calm in her white festive dress (put on front in front, and almost clean). Her little hand rests on the neck of a white fallow doe that ambles beside her. Their two auras mingle and overlap, the child's huge white mist and the doe's small green mist.

Both feel us watching. Both look our way, and start. They stop still, side by side, heads high. Their joined aura flares up. A long moment they exchange glances with us. Ynis raises a hand to brush back her loose, dark hair. Then they move gently away.

Merlin comments. "Despite all, I see you still have your magic white deer; that promises prosperity."

Merry says, "Their numbers began to rise. But this year they are seldom seen."

"Did maybe hunger diminish the white deer?"

"Nay! Folk would as soon eat their children as those deer."

"Ah, well. One bad year in ten bountiful . . ." Enchanter ripples.

Niviene remarks to me, "A wonderfully talented child. You must give thanks for her every day." If any other woman spoke, I would suspect envy in her voice.

"Aye, Niviene. I give thanks for so much!"

Giving thanks in my heart, I look out over Fair-Field. The Midsummer sun stands high. Now, smoke and folk are rising. The children who ran with the dogs have returned to their breakfast fires; the dogs circle, waiting for crumbs.

These are my folk. I am thankful to be theirs. Despite my dreadful secret, I am still their honored witch. I give thanks for the powers for which they value me. I give thanks for the world around me, summer-vibrant, for my body, my soul's home, already healing and rebuilding itself after the famine. I give deep thanks for my children.

Ynis's gesture just now, brushing back her hair, is Granny's gesture of mild surprise. It has a seductive look, unsettling in a child—and in a very old lady.

In his basket, Dace whimpers, stretches and wiggles pink toes. I gather him up in one arm and pull down my green gown.

Niviene murmurs, "He is not swaddled."

"Nay. My— I was advised against swaddling my children. It would bind up their spirits."

"Ah. Your beautiful daughter was never swaddled."

"Never."

Gently, she nods. "Where I come from, children are left unbound from birth. They go entirely free younger than your daughter. It troubles me to see one bound up in his cradle."

I swallow fear and whisper, "Where you come from . . . ?"

"Very far from here, Gwyneth." We let it go at that.

The men talk soft man talk, mumbling and snorting laughter. Niviene watches Dace and me. In any other woman's face those deep, watching eyes would signal envy.

MERLIN SONG

At Summerend, when ghosties go
Grieving and grumbling to and fro,
When food for them is spread on table,
Prayers prayed for them; and agile, able
Folk dare the dark, fearful of fable,
In mask and mien to fright the devil;
At Summerend, when rowdy revel
Reels in the road; but laughter's hollow,
And feebly flickers flame in tallow;
At Summerend was grim Gawain
Fevered to find his fated bane.
"I know not where the place may be,
This Chapel Green where waits the Knight.
I must be near there, brave to see,
Buckled and bold, by Christmas night.
I must be there on New Year morn,
To die before the year's well born,
Or for a coward be forgot,
Among the faint and failed my lot.
Merlin Mage, point me the way!
I must be there on New Year Day.
North?
You say North?
I must go North?
Not North! Not North! Not North!"

THE
GREEN
CHAPEL

"Lady Mary," prayed Gawain. "Queen of Heaven, Christ's holy Mother, guide me!"

He knelt in snowy dusk beside his chestnut charger, Gringolet. Thinner, much hungrier than when they set out, man and horse hung heads and turned backs to the moor wind.

"You know, Lady, the course of my travels. But you know it from heaven. Let me tell you from here on earth, how it has been.

"Lady, for weeks I have ridden north as Merlin bade me, not toward cursed Holy Oak and Satan's Dun, preserve me! But east of there. The Green Knight claimed to be known. 'Ask for the Green Chapel, you cannot fail to find me.' I have asked for the Green Chapel everywhere. Everywhere I meet with shrugs and shaken heads.

"At every ford I have found foes waiting, foul and fierce. I have struggled with wild men, with bear and bull and boar. Truly I know, you have preserved me! Had I not served you and your Son since boyhood, I would now be dead many times over.

"Yet, Lady, I am a King's Companion. These fights and struggles have not worried me much. For this journey I am well armed and was well provisioned.

"But now Christmas is past, and my provisions are long exhausted. Winter worries me—freezing rain, snow, and sleet. Half dead from cold I have slept many nights in my armor, sometimes under icicle caverns by hillside springs.

"Lady, in heaven you know no cold, no snow, no hun-

139

ger. Have you forgotten these small trials? Lady, mercifully remember and help me!"

Beside Gawain, Gringolet shifted and blew. His ears turned forward.

"Lady Mary! Show me the Green Chapel. If I cannot find it, that will not be my fault! Yet Merlin will never sing of me again. Men will call me coward.

"Finding it, I find Death and Honor.

"Lady, you know my Honor is besmirched. You know I broke a promise. I left my helpless love asleep in a cold cave on a barren moor like this one. You saw that from heaven, but here on earth it is still secret. It may be I have been led back up north here to atone for that very sin. As to that, you know the answer."

Gringolet stretched his snow-maned neck and whinnied. He pawed hard earth with an unshod front hoof. All four shoes were long lost on the moor.

"Lady Mary, I pray to you, lead me to the Green Chapel! Or at least to shelter for this night. I have not strength left to build a fire! Amen, dear Lady, Amen!"

Gawain looked up at the restless horse. "What ails you? Heh?"

Hope struck like a ray of heavenly light. "Angel Michael! You see something!"

Suddenly desperately strong, Gawain almost jumped up. Heedless of aching bone and worn-out muscle, he mounted Gringolet.

"Lady Mary! Queen of Heaven! I did not see that forest line before. And what is that, all white under dark trees?"

Gawain strained to see through fast-gathering, snowing dark. Quickly his trained eyes picked out the white shape, even to the twitch of ears and tail, the prance of slender legs.

"God's teeth, it's a white fallow deer! Maybe sent by Holy Mary to guide me. Or at least to stave off starvation!"

Not for the first time, Gawain galloped toward a tree line and a flitting white shadow.

SIR. (SAID INNER MIND.) *This hall seems odd. Strange. Outland.*

So. This is Outland. This is the north.

I liked it not from the outside. Hidden in forest. Thatch from rooftree to ground, like a peasant hut.

Worry, worry! Feel this good fire! Gawain hastened to stand close by it.

And not a sound from here, nor from the outbuildings! Silent as . . .

I smell pork!

Sir, I tell you true; when I saw this strange hall through the trees, I almost saw a fence of skulls around it. And that one-eyed servant who let us in . . .

He startled me, too. Looked almost familiar.

Aye, that's it! And the way he said, "Stand by the fire. Open no door." Why did he say that?

Look, I care not who or why. Just so they bring on the pork!

Never saw I hall so bare!

Gawain glanced about the large, very simple hall. He stood alone by a dug, unlined fire pit in the middle. Flickering firelight showed him a large trestle table set ready for dinner with two trenchers, two mugs, and burning candles. Other than this and two stools, the large room offered no furniture.

The dim hall was round, shaped like a summer pavilion or peasant hut. Carelessly laid thatch bunched down through a lattice of bent boughs. The floor-rushes covered trampled dirt. There were no windows.

Four closed doors there were: the front door, through which he had come; a door through which—even closed—came stomach-rending food smells; and two doors opposite each other.

Sir, I think this hall has been knocked together in a great hurry.

God-thank! Smell that roasting pork!

Sir, tremble not with eagerness! Conceal. Control. Preserve a seemly dignity.

Right. You are right. I will stand like a wooden statue.

That one-eyed fellow . . . Look you—what secret hides behind these doors?

I care not, so our stomach be filled! And, Mary be praised, feel that good fire! Holy Mary brought us here, remember. Worry no more.

Sir. On guard.

One of the opposite doors opened. The large, dark, fur-clad figure who waddled into firelight opened both arms wide and grinned through a bushy black beard. "A visitor! God's truth, we get few of those here! Be welcome, guest!"

He advanced upon Gawain. No taller, he yet outweighed Gawain as a bear outweighs a hound. Gawain was glad he did not actually embrace him as a bear might. They might both have toppled into the fire.

"I am Lord Bright, head of this house." A proud sweep of a pudgy, gloved hand indicated the round, bare room. "Come, guest, tell me your name!"

The smell of pork seeping through the back door overwhelmed Gawain. For a moment, he hardly knew his name.

Sir! Dignity! Courtesy!

He pulled himself together. "Lord, I am Gawain, Knight of the Round Table, King's Companion."

"Heh? What say, what say?" His rotund host took his elbow and marched him to the table. "Sit you here, Sir." Gawain crashed onto the proffered stool. "And I will sit here." Bright took the opposite stool. "You are Gawain Who?"

"I . . ." Gawain's head swam. "Knight of the Round Table . . ."

"And what table's that?"

". . . King's Companion . . ."

"To what king, Sir?"

The back door opened.

In marched the one-eyed servant with a blast of winter-night air. He bore the steaming, black-crackled pork in one trencher, breads in another. He slapped both trenchers on the table between host and guest, turned, and stomped out the door. In a moment he was back with two skin bottles of ale. He thumped these down and turned to leave again.

"Harrumph!" His master snorted through his beard.

The one-eyed servant paused, turned, and offered an awkward, hasty bow to each knight. Then he departed, apparently for good, banging the door behind him.

God's teeth! Never seen such sloppy service! What sort of lord can this Bright be?

Gawain heard neither his host's voice nor that of his Inner Mind. His being flowed from him and wrapped itself around the pork.

"Never mind all that now," Lord Bright boomed. He pushed the trencher toward Gawain. "Dig in, Sir! You've had a cold ride to get here."

"Now"—Lord Bright wiped his mouth and beard vigorously on his sleeve—"now, Sir . . . Gawain, I have a question for you."

Fed and warm, Gawain looked at his host with almost steady eyes. "I'll try to answer, Lord Bright."

"You came in here starved off the moor. I won't say drooping. Ha-ha! I'm glad to see you raise up now, like rain-crushed barley when the sun shines."

Gawain said a bit stiffly, "That is due to your hospitality, Lord Bright."

"Good! Ha-ha! But your spirit still lies crushed."

Caution! "My Lord, are you one of those who see the spirit?"

"See the spirit . . . Oh, no! Not me. No, I'm not one of those. But sorrow is plain to see in your face, Brother."

Gawain winced—first at the easy "Brother" spoken to a King's Companion and then to think that his sorrow was plain to see. He thought he had learned to mask it the moment the headless Green Knight thundered out of King's Hall.

Well. He had to ask the dread question, anyhow.

"My Lord . . ." He let Lord Bright refill his mug. This northern ale was altogether strong and strange, but his Lady Green of Doleful Memory had taught him to like it. "My Lord, you see not sorrow in my face, but the constraint of hard duty."

"Heh? Hah?" Lord Bright leaned forward, bristling interest.

"I came here to these parts in search of a hall called the Green Chapel. Do you know of it?"

Lord Bright cocked and scratched his head. "The Green Chapel. Ho-ho. Let me think. Meantime, why do you want this Green Chapel?"

"I must meet one there on New Year's morning. It is a matter of High Honor."

Reverently: "High Honor. Aha. Then I take it you will fight?"

"No, my lord. There will be no fight."

"But you said . . . High Honor . . ."

"I shall yield myself to the Knight of the Green Chapel."

Lord Bright stared. *"What?"*

In brief, bitter words Gawain explained. "A huge man, my Lord. Green entirely. Richly dressed and got up, and all in green. On a green horse."

Lord Bright's mouth gaped pink in his black beard.

"The severed head said, 'Men call me the Knight of the Green Chapel. Ask for the Green Chapel and you cannot fail to find me.' My lord, I have asked from Arthur's Dun to here, and I have failed to find it. Can you help me?"

Virgin Mother, let him know!

Queen of Heaven, let him not know! That will not be my fault.

Gawain reached for his mug.

Lord Bright winked one blue eye and bushy brow. "Brother, I think maybe I can."

Gawain set down the mug.

Lord Bright's beard wiggled and waggled. Then, "Aye, sir, I think I've just remembered. Not far from here is an old burial mound, you know the kind. Where a tribe buries its most honored dead. You know what I mean."

"Ah. . . Aye. A burial mound." Gawain's heart thumped slowly, loudly.

"Folk call this mound the Green Chapel. Don't know why. Ain't no greener than anyplace else.

"Anyhow. Now and then, fellow hangs around there. Fellow with an ax. All green, like you said. Huge. Fierce like an ogre. Maybe he is an ogre. Folk stay well away from him."

Gawain's breath slowed.

"Never saw no green horse, though."

"You've . . . seen this green man?"

"From a distance, Brother. No wish to see closer."

"God's teeth."

"Hah?"

"This can only be the Knight of the Green Chapel."

"Well, he could be a knight. Or a Fey phantom. Or a heathen God."

"And the mound is known as . . ."

"The Green Chapel, aye. And where might you find another green man?" Lord Bright raised his mug and slurped.

"This must be the place. And the man." Gawain gasped for breath. His heart slammed in his chest.

"Why don't you just stay on here? Plenty room." Lord Bright twinkled at him. "Then on New Year's morning—that's only four days from now—One-Eye will guide you to the Chapel."

"I . . . er . . . I thank you, my Lord."

(Truth, I never thought to find it. Despite the green ax hung up by Uncle's Caliburn, I thought the whole thing must have been some sort of dream. I never truly expected to meet a man who knew the Knight of the . . .) Gawain swallowed hard and straightened on his stool. "You are hospitable, my Lord!"

Lord Bright chuckled. "I'll wager you think you'll have a dull time here."

Gawain hardly heard. He concentrated on breathing.

"Sometimes we liven things up. Next three days I have a big hunt planned."

"Oh?"

"Never fear, I won't ask you to hunt! Can see you're saddle sore. You can rest up in yon guest chamber." Lord Bright nodded past Gawain to one of the mysterious closed doors. "Whole room all to yourself. Furnished like lady's bower.

"Oh. That reminds me. My lady can entertain you while I hunt."

Gawain heard that. Lady? This dismal, knocked-together "hall" boasted a lady? He had thought Lord Bright and One-Eye the only natives.

"In fact! Ha-ha!" Lord Bright thumped down his mug. "Tell me, guest, how does this plan take you? I go hunting. Anything I catch, I bring it home evening time, give it to you. You stay home here. Rest. Shine up your High Honor. (Twinkle.) Anything you catch, you give me, evening time. Would you call that a merry game?"

"Aye, my Lord." (Inside his swimming head, Gawain watched a real Green Knight heft his real green ax.)

"I'd call it a right entertainment, myself!"

"Aye, my Lord."

"Keep your mind off your troubles."

"Aye, my Lord . . ."

"So we're agreed? On both our Honor."

Gawain started. "My Lord?"

"Ha-ha, you weren't listening. Thought so. Look you, now. For the next three days I go hunting and give you my take. You entertain yourself, and my lady, and give me your take. Is that agreed?"

"Why . . . aye, my Lord."

"Agreed! Agreed!" Lord Bright's roar brought thatch bits drifting down from the roof like snow. "One-Eye! More ale!"

*S*IR, WAKE UP!

Heh?

A horn blast shattered dream. Neighs, shouts, and the tramp of hooves sounded on all sides. Gawain came wide awake in a rush.

Holy Michael! What . . .

Heavy eyelids tore themselves open. Bleary eyes took in blue-and-white-striped bedcurtains above and about. Spine stretched happily on a soft mattress.

Mary be thanked, I'm in a bed! In truth, a real bed! But what's that hunting horn blaring about?

Inner Mind said, *It's Lord Bright, Sir. Going hunting. Listen, here come the hounds.*

Ah. Lord Bright.

Dimly, Gawain remembered a round, dark face, bristling black beard, genial, rumbling voice: "I go hunting and give you my take . . ."

My host. Lord Bright, head of this house. Ah, aye!

He remembered coming upon this house last night at the end of dusk. It had loomed out of the dark woods, a round thatched hall with thatched outbuildings close by. A brigands' den. Or witches' shrine. *Was there not a fence adorned with skulls in front?*

Bushes, Sir. Snowcapped bushes.

Aye. He remembered the one-eyed servant admitting him, the dark silence of the bare hall, where only the snapping fire greeted him. Fire. Food. Bed!

God be thanked for this fine bed!

First in a while, Sir.

No wonder I slept like dead drunk . . .

First ale in a while. That northern stuff, too.

What am I doing here?

Sir, do you not remember? You have found the Green Chapel. It waits nearby.

God shield!

Gawain suppressed a mighty groan as the whole wheel of memory rolled into consciousness. Three days more to live. Three days more of light, shadow, dark, cold, heat, hunger, maybe even food. Three days more of being Gawain, guessed soul and known body, clothed in worldly respect, fame, and glory.

Take heart, Sir. Merlin will sing of you yet more grandly.

" 'Come to my chapel, or called coward be.
Knight of the Green Chapel, all men know me.
Seek me and find me; my chapel at morn.
Your head will my chapel fitly adorn.'
Gawain leaned on his ax, with Fey blood all green.
No grief or fear in his face to be seen,
No fear or grief in his heart to be found,
Gawain, the best knight that ever trod ground."

Hush, Fool! Let Merlin sing as he likes. Dead, I shall not hear him.

Gawain imagined his head sliced off—this dark-haired, noble-featured head, with its quick, hard grey eyes and all its thoughts roiling within, and memories, and Gawain-ness.

"Never another shall match his mien;
Gawain, the best knight that ever was seen."

He lay still and stiff, staring up at the blue and white stripes angling down. Just outside, the horn sounded again. Dogs answered, and there was a great tramp of hooves.

Somewhere in the woods about, boar and stag must hear this uproar. Heads must rise, ears flex, hearts thump. For the first time in his life, Gawain seemed to hear horn and hunt coming after him, and almost upon him. In fleeting vision he saw himself flee in front of the hounds, he who had always chased behind.

Maybe you could use these days to repent, Sir.
Repent!

Come, Sir. Famous you are, and well deserve to be. Sinless you are not.

Gawain let his eyelids sink shut. Small, remembered sins flitted through his skull. Childish lies told to Mother's cold face; a brother beaten up behind her kitchen house; a frightened slave girl in Uncle's Dun; anger; more anger.

(Anger was always my Cardinal Sin.)

After Pride, Sir.

Justified Pride is no sin! We cannot all be humble cowherds and cowards. Some of us are born to rule, and humility in such men may be itself a sin.

Sir, you are turned philosopher!

A girl lay asleep in a cave on a rainy moor. Gawain took her knife and their pony, and stole away.

He groaned aloud. *Truth, for that one great sin I deserve the Green Chapel! Pray God Merlin and his ilk never find out!*

Pray. Good idea, Sir.

Horn and hounds blaring, the hunt outside rumbled away.

With aching effort, Gawain rolled out of bed. Naked and freezing, he knelt on the floor and prayed softly, aloud. "Holy Mary! Ask your Son's forgiveness for my great sin. You know how often, how bitterly, I have repented it."

He repeated the prayer twice, then tried to stand up. *Oof! My head! How much ale did the good Lord Bright pour down me?*

Momentarily flopped on the floor, he remembered Lord Bright's words. "I go hunting and give you my take. You entertain yourself and give me your take. On both our Honor."

Strange. What can I take here in his hall, that I should give him?

Well, Sir. If you take nothing, you need give nothing.

*Right. But how did I come to this sad pass, that I can
hardly lift myself off the floor?*

Sir, you are mightily exhausted.

Aye. In bone, muscle, and innards.

*Climb back into bed, Sir. Lord Bright himself advised
that.*

Dizzy and gasping, Gawain hauled himself back into
the warm bed within the warm curtains. Never since childhood had he been ill—only wounded—and it never oc-
curred to him that he might be ill now. Gratefully, he
closed his eyes . . .

Sir! Wake up!

Heh? Gawain started awake.

Someone at your door.

Right. A slight sound at the door.

Spy, Sir!

Gawain opened one eye and lifted a corner of curtain.

He spied while softly, the door opened. Softly, a
woman entered.

Tall and lean, she was gowned and wimpled in rose-
dyed wool that let no strand of hair show. In one hand she
carried a tankard.

Breakfast!

But this woman was no servant, come to bring ale and
take away the chamber pot. Jewels gleamed green on
wrists and fingers and neck. A fine gauze veil shadowed
half her face, and about her slender waist wound a green
lace girdle, shot with gold. She stood and moved with a
pride that somehow seemed almost familiar . . . but
could not be familiar. Could it?

Head swimming, at a loss for right word or action,
Gawain dropped the curtain corner and pretended sleep.

He heard the soft *snick* of the door closing, and a hasp
drawn across. He heard a whisper of swaying robe and
curtain swept aside. Morning light touched his face. He

breathed slowly and relaxed his eyelids, as he had learned to fool Nurse long ago in Mother's house. Then after Nurse went away, thinking her charges asleep, he and his brothers would jump out of bed . . .

He felt the woman—the lady—standing there over him. He felt her keen gaze.

To his shock, he felt the bed depress slightly as she sat down beside him. He drowned in heady perfume and a tingling physical awareness.

By Saint John, who can this be?

You know, Sir. Lady Bright. Lord Bright mentioned her at dinner.

God's teeth! I'm expected to entertain her!

Early to start.

Maybe she wants to entertain me! What shall I do?

Wake up, Sir. For courtesy.

Gawain opened his eyes and saw the lady smiling down at him. This close she was handsome, if a bit thin. Maybe the half veil was a good idea. Her lower face looked somewhat coarse. Peasantish.

But her looks hardly mattered. Sensuality surrounded her like perfume, like a pool in which she stood thigh-deep, gazing out invitingly.

(—And I thought I was too tired to feel like this!)

In a sweet, almost southern voice—though northernly accented—she said, "Good morning, Sir Gawain! I have captured you, and I shall bind you in your bed!"

He smiled up at her. "Good morning, Lady. I yield and ask for grace."

They smiled together. She held out the tankard she carried. He sat up to drink. The warm, overly strong ale assaulted his tongue. "I am Lady Bright, your hostess. I am here to entertain you while my lord hunts."

Gawain gulped. "Lady, let me get up and dress. Then

we can talk comfortably." He made a weak motion to rise. Her ringed hand flashed to press down his shoulder.

"Oh, no, Sir! Nay, in truth, you shall not rise from your bed. I mean to sit here and talk with my captured knight. For I know who you are."

"Why Lady, I am—"

"I know you are Sir Gawain of the Round Table, King's Companion and nephew, of whom bards sing—even the great Merlin—and who is honored far and wide and everywhere he rides."

"Well . . ." Gawain felt the accustomed pleasure of praise warm face and body.

"Now I have you in my house!" she continued. "Drink, Sir Gawain." He drank again. "Now you and I are alone, and the door shut, and the hasp drawn, and my lord and his men gone hunting."

"Aye, Lady?" Gawain was uneasily reminded of a tale Lancelot told, of being taken asleep in a wood by three Fey ladies and their enchantment-enslaved knights. This one lady needed no knights or enchantment! Her perfume, of body and mind, was enchantment enough.

"So! Since I have in my hands him whom all the world loves, I mean to use my time well while it lasts." She took the tankard from him and set it on the floor. Very simply she said, "You are welcome to my body. I am here to serve you."

What!

So? This is not the first woman to creep to your bed. Look you not so abashed!

Body agreed eagerly. But Gawain thought, *God shield, this lady is Lord Bright's wedded wife! Honor absolutely forbids.*

He said, "In good faith . . . I think . . ."

"Yes?"

He collected his wandering tongue and thoughts. "In

good faith, I think you mistake me for some other man. I am . . ." He swallowed and managed unfamiliar words. "I am unworthy of the high honor you show me. By God, Lady, in any other way I can serve you . . . it would be pure joy."

"There are ladies enough in the world who would give much treasure and gold to have you in their hands, as I have you now! Sir Gawain, I would gladly do anything for you."

"Lady, Mary save you! I admire your generosity. But it is I who should serve you."

"I think otherwise. For believe me, if I were the richest woman in the world and could choose any lover I liked, for your beauty and fame and courtesy I would choose you."

"You have already chosen your lord well." Gawain thought of Lord Bright, riding hearty and hale now in the woods, and this tall, thin lady reeking of attraction, together. He thought he had spoken right; truly, they made a good pair. "But I am very proud of the worth you put on me . . ." He was falling asleep as he talked! That was strong ale in that tankard. "I will be your knight, Lady, and take you for my sovereign . . ."

She stood up and away. From cracked-open eyelids he saw her stand against morning light, holding the bed-curtain back. To his relief, the demanding pressure of her attraction moved a little away.

"I wonder if you really are Sir Gawain, King's Companion!"

"Lady, why so?" (Could he have failed in courtesy or shown weakness?)

"From what I have heard of Sir Gawain, he would never dally so long with a lady without asking a kiss!"

Gawain silently cursed the inventions of imaginative minstrels. But . . . a kiss. One harmless kiss.

Groggily, Gawain drew himself up in the bed. "Lady, gladly will I kiss you at your command, for—"

She fell upon him.

GAWAIN DREAMED HIS OWN praises.

Harmless kiss, by God! And I withstood it. I sent her away with pious words, God save you, Mary keep you. Merlin will never sing of this, but I will die knowing my own true, unstained worth. I am indeed Sir Gawain of the Round Table, King's Companion; I am more truly he than I knew! I will shine in heaven like a star, like a shield burnished past shining—

Sir.

Leave me alone.

Sir, something is strange here. I wonder if we are bewitched.

Heh? Gawain cracked open one eye.

Consider, Sir. Listen to this. Suppose Merlin sang you this story: A white doe leads us from dusky moor to forest hall. Here we find three persons Lord Bright, his crazed wife, and his servant One-Eye. No host of knights, squires, pages, cooks—

Did we not hear a hunt depart, just now?

We heard it. We did not see it.

Hmmm. True.

Consider farther. Lord Bright dines with you alone and makes you a bargain.

Gawain cracked the other eye. *Bargain! God's teeth! When he comes home tonight, what do I give him? A kiss?*

That's what you took in his house.

I did not take it. It was freely given . . . very freely.

Mary's veil, what a kiss! Gawain paused to savor the memory. *But if Lord Bright learns of this, he will beat his wife! I would not bring that about. That would be . . . unknightly.*

Fear not overmuch, Sir. He must know her for what she is, crazed or wanton. You cannot be the first guest she has kissed!

By Saint Giles, no!

But Sir, all these strangenesses . . . I suspect these folk are Fey, and have us prisoned in enchantment.

Hah?

I suspect this is no forest hall, but an oak grove, of the type we know well already; no bed, but a bank of oak leaves.

No—

Pshaugh! Leave off your suspicions.

Consider—

No more! If this bed be a bank of leaves, it is the warmest, softest bank I ever slept upon . . .

Sir—

For God's love! If we are enchanted, we are enchanted. We might as well die in these leaves, this bed, as in the Green Chapel. We will die easier, here!

Gawain pulled the wool blankets over his bare shoulders and slept.

AT FIRST DARK, HORNS, shouts, and barks announced the return of the hunt.

Weak and dizzy, Gawain met Lady Bright by the hall fire, even as One-Eye silently piled on wood. Quickly, briskly he worked, snapping twigs and rolling logs, looking nowhere but to the rising fire.

For the first time in a season, Gawain wore soft indoor

garments—embroidered slippers, hose, long maroon tunic and cloak—none of them his own. Waking in the afternoon, he had found these on the stool where his lousy, frost-cracked clothes and mail had lain. More important, his sword was gone.

Inner Mind had counseled, *Uncle does not allow knights to wear swords at his table, either. When you leave, your own clothes, mail, lice, and sword will surely be brought you.*

("Leave!" The word had given Gawain a sudden, sharp neckache. To salve it, he had drunk deeply of the full tankard left beside the stool.)

Lady Bright fairly glowed in leaping firelight. Her scarlet gown and wimple drank light, gold bracelets and rings reflected light. Beneath her half veil her handsome (if somewhat coarse) features betrayed no fear; but Gawain sensed tension in her proud stance. He said quickly, softly, "Lady. I am Honor-bound to give your lord what I have found in his house this day."

She smiled gently into his face. Slightly surprised, he noticed they were nearly the same height. "Dear Sir Gawain!" she answered low, "well I know how you value your Honor. Whatever you have found in my lord's house, give to him with my blessing."

Gawain scented her perfume and felt again the mighty magic of her attraction. He thought, *Lord Bright may beat her . . . might kill her . . .*

But I doubt it, Sir. Her charms are a strong shield.

Hooves thundered around the flimsy hall. Thatch fell in dusty clumps through the roof-lattice. The door burst open.

Lord Bright filled the doorway. With knife bristling, rough hunting garb, and wild beard bloodied, he looked a likely wife-killer. White-faced Lady Bright gave him a calm glance.

"Ho, ho, honored guest!" Lord Bright cast huge arms wide and waddled toward Gawain. "I've brought you gifts and more gifts! Did you rest well, guest?"

Two great black hounds with bloodied jaws burst in after Lord Bright. Growling like bears, they trotted around the fire pit.

"My Lord, I rested quite well—"

"Good! Good! Come out here now and see what I have for you!" A powerful paw descended on Gawain's shoulder and urged him to the door. Shivering in his light tunic, Gawain stepped out into cold darkness.

A cheerful fire burned among outbuildings on the clearing's edge. Silhouettes of men and dogs milled around it. By the door a groom held a torch. Its ragged red light shifted over a second groom, two blowing, sweat-shiny pack ponies, and their burdens of bleeding meat.

"You should have come!" Lord Bright roared. "You should have heard our horns, chased our chase!"

The two black hounds bounded about the ponies' feet, snapping up at the meat. One hound leaped against Lord Bright. He caught and kneaded its ears with gloved fingers as a baker kneads bread, to its whining delight. The ponies stamped and stirred, unhappy with the heavy, wreathing blood smell.

Gawain folded his arms tight against the cold and stood astraddle, lest his knees knock.

"We let the antlered harts and bucks go by." Lord Bright almost sang like a bard. "No stringy, worn-out meat for us! We drove the hinds and does down to the water. A great run, Sir! Horn and hound! Sun and wind! Bump and thump! Ech, you should have come!"

Gawain locked his jaws lest the complaint of his chattering teeth be heard. Not much danger there. Voices of men and dogs rose now from the fire among the huts. And Lord Bright thought only of his hunt.

"Down at the water we had men and hounds waiting, you know. Skilled and strong. So fast, they grabbed the deer in an eyeblink. Pulled 'em down. Ripped 'em up. In a breath. You should have seen how fast they butchered! All done there by the water." Jovially, Lord Bright slapped a sack of offal. "Sorted out on the spot. No mess here!"

"My Lord," Gawain managed politely between chattering teeth, "I c-c-c-congratulate your hunt!"

"Look here!" Lord Bright lifted an edge of raw, winter-grey hide. "Good as you've seen, I'll wager. And look how skillfully done, not a cut on it. Top speed."

"I . . . c-c-c-congratulate . . ."

"And all this, guest, is for you!" Lord Bright hurled the hound away and grabbed Gawain to his chest. "This is my own take, for my own use—three deer! Which I give you here and now, according to our covenant."

"Thank you, my . . . L-L-L-ord. Now I have something to give you . . . to return some p-p-part of your hospitality."

"Aye! I'll wager that here at home you have taken something worth more than all this!"

"I . . . m-m-m-meant to say, my Lord . . . I return this, your gift of m-m-meat, for your later feasting."

"Hah! Then shall we feast together, Sir Gawain. Later."

"Ah, no, my Lord. I d-d-doubt that I shall ever feast again."

"Come, man!" Lord Bright clapped Gawain's two shoulders and shook him back and forth. "No need for such gloom! Sad thought brings sadness. Like the song says, *Never mind mourning. Let her follow you.* Ech, you are cold!"

Gawain could no longer conceal his agony of cold. Teeth and knees and shudders proclaimed it.

"I forgot, you are not winter-dressed. Come inside, guest! Quick, by the fire!"

159

The fire burned high. Lady Bright stood in its light like a scarlet-painted church statue. Her face seemed blank, feelingless, in the shadow of her short veil. One-Eye had gone.

Gawain did not let himself stride directly to the fire, hold out his hands, or spread his stiff-frozen gown to it. He stopped beside Lord Bright, close to the table. The two black dogs brushed between them, ran straight to the fire pit, and flopped beside it.

"Now, guest!" Lord Bright barked cheerfully. "My gift! What you have taken today in my house is mine, by covenant!"

With an effort, Gawain did not glance Lady Bright's way. Somewhere in his misty head he had already decided that if Lord Bright threatened this wild, childish woman, he would intervene. He would defend her with his bare hands.

That decision made, he turned to Lord Bright, laid icy hands on his shoulders and kissed him once, square on his surprisingly soft lips.

Gawain stood away.

One still moment, his eyes met Lord Bright's open, serious gaze. He felt that in that moment he sank, or rose, into reality and faced the true Lord Bright, who wore his brusque, north-wind character like a mask. The moment passed.

"By Saint John!" Lord Bright rubbed off Gawain's kiss with a bloody glove. "I'll wager you did not take that treasure by resting all day! Where in God's name did you find it?"

Gawain held himself erect, despite chilled bones and aching head. "My Lord, what true knight betrays a kiss? Where I come from, such matters are secret."

"Ech, that's true here, too. Very true, Sir! And you are Honorable to remember it." Lord Bright turned slightly toward his silent, motionless lady. "Wife!" he shouted like a peasant. "Order up the dinner!"

All begrimed as he was, he strode to the table and crashed onto a stool. At his gesture, Gawain followed suit.

God's teeth, Sir! He means to eat like this. No wash, no comb! Bloody gloves. The man's a lord one moment, a knave the next.

This is the north. We know not its ways.

Now at last Gawain let his eyes stray to Lady Bright.

Slow and proud, she turned away and drifted to the back door.

I swear, I've known someone who walked like that! Somewhere. Somewhen.

She opened the door and called sweetly out into the dark. Then she slipped through herself and disappeared.

In marched One-Eye, piled trenchers in both hands. The two black dogs leaped up as he passed them and followed the trail of scent to the table. One-Eye slammed down the trenchers, went back to the fire for light, and lit the table candles. For the second time Gawain faced his host alone, across candlelight and food.

One-Eye brought tankards of ale, placed one before each knight, and departed unceremoniously. This time Lord Bright made no remark upon his rude service, demanded no parting bow.

Both starved knights fell to.

IN GAWAIN'S DREAM, LORD Bright raised his ruddy, beard-bushed face and smiled. In a weird, heavy accent he said, "As I am True Knight, I swear, I will send you to the Green

Chapel at New Year's daybreak. For I have tested you and found you faithful."

His dream-smile widened to an ogre's grin. His ruddy face turned green. An ax whooshed down past Gawain's closed eyes—which shot wide open.

Pounding heart. Morning light on blue and white bedcurtains. A silky rustle.

"Man!" said a sweet southern voice above him. "How can you sleep so on such a bright morning? The hunt just departed, and you never stirred!" Lady Bright leaned over the bed; one jeweled hand held back the curtain, one offered ale. "Drink, Sir Gawain." Gracious smile. Outstretched tankard.

Gawain's heart still thumped, unhappy with the whooshing ax he had dreamed. He sighed, wiped dreams from his eyes with the heels of his hands, sat up.

"Drink to our morning, dear Sir."

Gawain drank.

"Drink deeper, for I would enjoy this fine, clear morning with the finest knight in the world!" He swallowed again.

She bent to take back the tankard. Grasping it, she kissed his mouth. "Sir, let me tell you I am cold standing here! I'll wager your bed is warm with wool, and fur, and your own lively self. Hold you the tankard while . . . " Lady Bright lifted the bedclothes and popped quietly in beside Gawain.

Perfumes of dead summers overwhelmed confused senses. *God's bones! but she must be beautiful under gown and veil!*

Magical beauty haloed her peasant-seeming hands, her face glimpsed in veil-shadow. Under that concealing wimple, Gawain knew, her hair would be rich, fairy-spun gold. Under the rose silk gown . . .

162

*By Angel Michael, why not? If not now, when? Two days
more and I die. Die, for God's love!*

Sir, wait! Sir, consider your sacred honor!

("I have tested you," said Lord Bright, "and found you
true.")

Lady Bright arranged pillows at both their backs and
plumped herself restfully against them. With a smile like
Springtime's own, she took the tankard from him, sipped,
and handed it back.

Gawain fought himself. His hands rose toward her,
sank back. His breath sped, slowed.

She said, "Sir Gawain, I think you must have a lady
friend of whom the songs tell not."

"Why . . . why do you think that, Lady?" His throat
closed sorely upon the words.

"Believe me, not many men would lie so gently beside
me!"

"Lady, that is certain truth. And I mean no discour-
tesy—"

"I think only a man whose heart was given away already, only one who could not even see me, or feel me,
because his mind was bent on his beloved . . ."

"Lady, Honor is my beloved. You are wed to my host,
the generous Lord Bright—"

"Honor! Nay, you have a true love, Sir! I know the
signs. Give me another sip."

"Keep the ale with you."

"Nay, Sir, we share this morning drink!" She handed it
back with some small force, so that he had to hold or spill
it.

He said, "To answer you, no; I have no lady love. Nor
shall I ever have one, now."

She laid her head on his shoulder. Her warmth came
around him like protection. "My lord told me a strange, sad
tale of you."

"I am to die in two days."

"Such a dreadful fate, to die because of a Yuletide game!" Her hand moved softly on his bare chest. "That such a fine man should be lost to the world through a game! I could well weep. But I would rather make you merry, dear Sir. Do you know the new song?"

Into his neck, stirring his beard, she sang.

> *"Mirth's a merry maiden*
> *To follow and pursue.*
> *Never mind Mourning.*
> *Let her follow you."*

Deeply, then, she sighed. "I love you, Sir Gawain of High Honor."

"Lady," he confessed, love-swollen throughout, "I love you!" Firmly he pushed aside her hand and straightened up. He drank one last, deep swallow for strength and said, "I love you with all my heart, and desire you with all my body. But this love we share must go no farther, for Honor forbids. You are my good host's wife."

Under the little veil, her eyes went wide. She straightened beside him, staring at him, awestruck, through her veil. "Honor forbids . . . I would not have believed it."

"God forbids, Lady. In the name of all that is right—"

"You are truly that determined, Sir?"

He said desperately, honestly, with no courtly grace, "I am about to die. What I tell you now is true. I am determined to die with Honor. Though refusing you is the hardest thing I have ever done."

"Give me the tankard, Dear." She took and set it on the floor. "Kiss me once."

"Lady, I am deter—"

The kiss was long and deep.

Sadly, then, she said, "I see truly we will make no merry today. I will go."

"Lady! If in truth you love me kindly, come you not back here!"

AGAIN, BEDCURTAINS RUSTLED. *Nay, not the lovely Lady Bright, God shield!*

Gawain cracked open a bleary eye. Subdued, indoor noon light leaned in the curtain-crack, and a dark-cloaked, hooded figure. White hair bloomed under the hood, white beard peeped through the cloak.

"Mage Merlin!"

"Son Gawain, how do you here?"

The gentle voice both calmed and stirred Gawain. To his horror, he felt tears rise in his throat. He swallowed them back. "Not well, Mage! Not well. Come you to cure me?"

"Maybe."

"Are you truly here? Or do you travel in spirit?"

Merlin stood silent. Then, "In what way are you not well, Sir Gawain?"

"In truth, I know not. I am dizzy, all the time. I am never sure if what I see is real or dream. Like yourself, now."

"You have come a long, cold way; you slept under icicle-falls. You fought bear and boar and brigand. Many a day you have gone hungry."

"True, Mage. I am tired."

Merlin nodded deeply. "Tired!"

"But I think it is more. I think maybe I am . . . bewitched."

"Bewitched?"

"Enchanted. Tell me, Merlin, do I truly lie here in a warm bed?"

"What do you think?"

"It might be only a heap of leaves . . . in an oak grove . . . I might be frozen dead and dreaming in spirit."

Merlin smiled in his beard. "You imagine wildly, Gawain!"

"Merlin, if you are truly yourself . . . and here . . . heal me!"

"So now once more you are ill. Not enchanted."

"I know not what to think!"

"Have you thought you might be drugged?"

Gawain sat bolt upright. "Drugged!"

Visions of tankards swam in his head. "All that northern ale! She keeps pressing it on me— God's teeth! I'll drink not a drop more of that!"

"A good way to start your cure." Merlin dropped the curtain back in place.

"Mage Merlin! Leave me not alone . . . " Gawain snatched the curtain aside. As he suspected, Merlin was gone. A handful of dust drifted where he had stood, in a shaft of light from the ill-thatched roof.

Head in a whirl, Gawain lay back on the pillows.

(Somewhere not far off, a young child cried. Gawain listened, interested to hear some sound from the usually silent world outside.)

Think this through.

Lord Bright is a right good knight. Stupid he may be, to leave his wild lady all day with a guest. But he would never drug a guest! If he wished me harm, he would give me back my sword and use his.

Swordless women resort to magic, tricks, and drugs. This must be the work of lovely Lady Bright. Lady Bright, who seems so sweetly crazed, may well be a witch. Witches abound here in the pagan north. Let me not forget, that's where I am. And where I was once before this.

By Saint George! She must truly want me!

On that thought, Gawain smiled and almost slept; but first he leaned down to the bedside tankard and knocked it halfway across the floor, spilling poison all the way.

HORN AND HOUND ANNOUNCED the hunt's return. Silent One-Eye built up the fire. Six yards apart, Gawain and Lady Bright faced the door.

Thunder of hooves; victory halloes. The door burst open.

In marched Lord Bright, bearing a heavy object aloft in both gloved hands. Striding into firelight, he fairly dripped blood and filth. Lady Bright gathered her gown and took a broad step away. Gawain might have followed suit, but after all, his soft, indoor garments belonged to Lord Bright. Let him be-grime them if he chose. Surprisingly undizzy, bones newly firm, Gawain stood his ground.

Before the door closed, Bright's two black dogs trotted in and bounded to the fire.

Grinning and stinking, Lord Bright marched up to Gawain and presented his burden: the grinning, severed head of a huge boar, wrapped in a net of vines for easy handling.

"My take, guest! For you!"

Gawain looked down at slitted, blood-clogged eyes and stout, froth-slimed tusks. He did not quite retch.

Highly thoughtless gift, Inner Mind said faintly. *Unconsidered. One head for another . . . !*

"Meat's out back at the kitchens," Lord Bright bellowed merrily. "Didn't think you'd want to handle that."

167

"As before, my Lord—"

"We'll feast on that together, eh? At a better time."

"Aye, my Lord." No need to remind or explain.

"But this, you can look at this while you eat!" Lord Bright swung about, strode to the table and set the boar's head in the middle. "One-Eye! Lights here!"

One-Eye ran across with a taper and lit all the table candles. Now the head swam in flickering light: dead eyes, useless tusks, foamed bristles, furious snarl.

"More that way." Lord Bright pointed at Gawain's waiting stool. "Turn it that way, man! So it looks at its new owner." One-Eye pointed the thick-slimed snout that way.

"I'll wager you've stuck a good count of boars in your time, Brother." Bright clapped and rubbed gloved hands together. "Can't find a Saxon, stick a boar, eh? Next best sport." Gawain smiled but did not need to answer. Bright rushed on, "But you should have been there, this hunt!

"He sat in his thicket, see, till the dogs came almost upon him. That's what they say, I was farther back. Then he rushed out and off, all the dogs after, all the men after, till none of 'em could run a step more.

"He comes to river-ford, steep bank. Backs himself into the bank." Lord Bright acted the boar's part, swinging from side to side and glaring, back against the table. "Paws the ground." Lord Bright "pawed" the rush-strewn earth floor. "Snarls. Men stand all around. Don't dare go for him."

The two black dogs left the fire to watch their master's act. Heads cocked, ears twitched. Tails stiffened.

"See, Sir, we know him. Done damage before now. Some of us bear old scars from those tusks." He nodded respect to the candlelit head. "So they all wait for me.

"Me, I ride up. Right quick I jump down. Draw dagger." Lord Bright's dagger rasped from sheath to fist. "Go for him."

A black dog uttered a sharp bark.

"He runs into ford. Turns. Snarls." Lord Bright snarled ferociously. Yellow teeth gleamed in black beard.

Both dogs growled.

"We close right there, Sir. In the water."

"I come up, see where to strike. Here, Sir." Bright jabbed a thumb into the base of his own burly throat. "Aim. Hit him to the hilt." Bright stabbed the air.

The black dogs sprang about, yelping.

"When they butcher, they find his heart clear sundered. But that don't stop him. Runs full tilt, clear across ford. Dogs catch him on bank. Worry him dead. Like he weren't dead already."

Panting slightly, Lord Bright sheathed his dagger. Noticed the dogs. "Git!" They continued to spring and yelp. He gave them a quick hand signal. They stopped mid-bark. "Go!" Bright pointed to the fireplace; ears and tails low, both dogs instantly slunk there and sat down like statues.

"Well, Sir!" Lord Bright turned snapping eyes to Gawain. "That's my story."

Truly impressed, Gawain said politely, "My Lord, I only wish I had been with you."

"Ech, we know you need your rest! Got your own hunt coming up."

"Aye, my Lord." A grim reminder. For a moment, hearing Lord Bright's tale, Gawain had almost forgotten the Green Chapel, now only one day ahead.

"So! You get my boar's head, and welcome to it! But now, what of your take?"

"My Lord?" Gawain's newly sober mind reeled into a new thought-path.

"I'm to get whatever you took here in my house. Remember?"

Gawain paused to remember what, exactly, he had

169

taken. Or had been given. "Aye, my Lord." He stepped up to Lord Bright.

Sober, he no longer feared much for foolish Lady Bright. Her husband must surely know her well. They might even be playing this game together, two cats with one mouse between them. Lord Bright would never do a guest actual, treacherous harm. But such a merry game would hardly besmirch his honor.

Soberly, Gawain kissed Lord Bright's sensitive, moist mouth; once, twice. And stepped back.

"Hah!" As before, Bright wiped the kisses away on his glove. "Two of them, this time! I think you have the better of me, guest. With such trade you'll soon be rich! Wife!" He roared, loud enough to be heard through the back door and bring thatch wisping down. "Wife! Dinner!"

Watch this, Inner Mind whispered. *Watch him eat with his gloves on. Why do you think he never takes them off?*

Doubtless his hands are deformed.

Or sliced off by an enemy, and he has only hooks.

Something like that. Hush. Here comes dinner.

Even as Lord Bright plunked himself down, bloody gloved hands spread wide on the board, One-Eye advanced through the back door in a cloud of roast-meat steam.

THE DEPARTING HUNT RUSHED rumbling away. Gawain came stark awake. *Third hunt. Third morning. Tomorrow—God shield!*

Dread froze him where he lay, frosted his bowels, iced his eyes shut. *Tomorrow I ride out with One-Eye to find the Green Chapel, and the Fey Green Knight who waits there, grinning, great green ax in hand. Tomorrow I feel that ax;*

and after that, nothing more. No thing, good or ill, forever-more, till Christ returns. God's teeth! I'd best drink Lady Bright's dizzy potion again. Better be half asleep than awake to this!

Inner Mind whispered, *Sir. Be you afraid?*

Gawain ground his teeth. *For sure I am afraid! Knight I am, and of the Round Table, and King's Companion; but Man I am also.*

Let it be so, Sir.

Eh? What say?

Let you be afraid. Fear is no sin.

Right! Gawain opened clenched eyelids. *God and Mary will not blame me.*

But fear is dishonorable in the world's eyes.

Fear that shows.

For one more day, Sir, let show no sign of fear.

Aye. No sign of fear.

Can you do that, Sir?

Gawain sat up in bed. He found his head wonderfully clear, his body rugged again, so quickly action-ready!

I am Gawain, King's Companion. For two cold moons I have ridden alone, eagerly hunting my death. I have battled, killed enemies, hunted boars three times bigger than Lord Bright's. I have traveled in barbarous parts. I have lain with women . . . I have sinned.

(Gawain knelt over sleeping Lady Green in the rain-cold cave. He took her knife.)

I used it not! I left her alive.

And asleep, and far from home.

Not so far from home as myself!

So you took the pony. And you lived to tell the tale, or one like it.

I lived. Unhappily.

You feel Dishonored.

Worse.

What can be worse than Dishonor?

Loss. Loss can be even worse than that.

The loss of . . . Come, Sir. On this third day we may as well be honest. The loss of . . .

Love.

You loved Lady Green.

I love Lady Green.

Who is most likely dead.

Not . . . necessarily. She's . . . strong.

But you would never see her again, even if you lived.

That was why I feared not the Green Knight . . . enough. Almost, I welcomed his weird challenge.

You tired of life!

I tired of lurking, hidden Dishonor. I tired of . . . loneliness.

There, Sir. It's all out at last. As a sick man finds health in vomiting, a sinner finds wholeness in confession, especially to himself.

Ha. Ha-ha! Witty, are you!

Bear witness. You do find wholeness. You see yourself clear.

Aye. I see myself hardly worth my own mourning!

Good. Let us now cease to mourn and mope.

What shall we do, this last day?

Act brave. Give the world a song, a story, it will never forget.

By God! That shall we do!

A cascade of new energy melted the ice of fear. Gawain fairly leaped out of bed and ripped aside the warm bedcurtains. His body met the winter morning with vigorous shivers and shudders, shaking off cold as a hound shakes off water. He found the chamber pot, and then "his" clothes. (*Tonight I must remind Lord Bright of my sword.*)

What can have happened to stubborn Lady Bright? She should be in here by now, cooing and rustling!

172

Let us go find her, Sir. Give her a tale to tell the world,
how Sir Gawain of the Round Table laughed away his last
day of life.

Let Merlin sing!

Gawain flung the chamber door open.

The shabby "hall" stretched away, empty and still.
One-Eye must have labored here lately; fire leaped in the
pit. Gawain went to stand in the warm and survey the pov-
erty-frozen room.

Daylight filtered down through smokehole and thatch;
also, occasional snowflakes.

If this is not an enchanted oak grove, it's the next thing
to it. Can't be much colder.

Beside the sagging boar head on the table stood a tankard, doubtless full, waiting.

Oh, no!

In four long strides Gawain reached the table. His fist
sent the tankard flying, drugged ale raining.

No more of that! I am Gawain, Knight—

Creak.

Sir, beware!

He swung about. Lord Bright's forbidden private door
drifted open.

There like a tall, slender rosebush swayed Lady Bright,
scarlet-gowned and green-girdled. In both square, bony
hands she lifted her scarlet wimple high, about to lower it
over head and shoulders. Once in place it would com-
pletely conceal the long, looped braid of rich red hair that
now flamed like a painted saint's halo about her head. For
the first time Gawain saw her whole face, startlingly pale
and thin; but, God! how well remembered!

Lady Green did not expect to meet Gawain here in the
hall. He was supposed to lie in drugged sleep behind blue-
and-white-striped bedcurtains in the next chamber. She expected to settle and fasten her wimple, take up the tankard

One-Eye had left on the table, and rustle through Gawain's door, shutting the hasp with a half-audible *snick*.

But here he stood, solidly erect in morning light, fully conscious grey eyes trained on her.

She started like a doe, all trembly-stiff.

HOLY GODDESS, HE KNOWS me!

Recognition widens his hard, grey eyes, now fully awake. Right hand leaps left to where sword should hang. Thank all Gods, I hid the sword away.

But this is only his instant answer to surprise. Had he the sword there to hand, he would not draw it. Because he loves me. My love loves me.

In his beloved eyes I see my own sorrow, my own loss and loneliness; all the grief I thought too heavy to bear, without the dark-shining shield of anger—he has known all that, too.

His hands lift up, amazed. Astonishment lights his face like moonlight; then joy sweeps across like sunlight. He comes to me. Across the rush-strewn, snow-speckled hall he strides, arms wide, orange aura wide-aflame.

Behind him, my Demon swirls like black smoke.

Gawain, my own Sir Gawain of the Round Table, May King, strides upon me. My own arms lift and open without my will. I sway and fall into his arms.

We clasp. We hug, embrace, teeter, reel. Wide and strong his chest, warm and hard his arms. I fold myself into him, nestle my face in the pulsing hollow of his throat. As a grouse creeps into grass and disappears like dappled shadow, so my soul creeps into his and folds her wings.

Long later, I open my eyes.

We sway beside the fire pit. Three stumbles more and we would fall in.

The boar head has somehow left the table. It hangs now in air over Gawain's right shoulder. I could reach up and touch it.

Froth- and sweat-slimed, it grins wide and wider. Its tusks drip blood. Its slitted eyes open. It winks.

Holy Gods, it is my Demon! The Demon who has lived in me, fed on my anger, fed my anger, while the sun wheeled once, and again half a year.

That I should have harbored this horror, unseeing! Even as I nursed my sweet Dace and tended my Ynis! Even as I advised and healed my Folk and wove good spells for them. That this monstrous Evil should have lived in my aura! Merlin and Niviene saw it. Merry saw it. Granny saw it. Why did they not turn from me as from plague?

I cry, "Go! Go, leave me!"

Gawain's arms loosen about me.

"Not you, Love! Not you! I never meant you!" I hug him tighter, squeeze my eyes back shut. We reel again, away from the fire. Now I am conscious enough to steer us.

When I look again we are backed against the table, wrapped closer together than mating serpents. The boar head sits once more on the table, safely dead.

We roll, sink, and fall away. We land on hard, rush-strewn earth between fire and table. Panting, we loosen our grip. Both of us gasp the same silly words: "Dear . . . Love . . . Sweetheart . . ." We draw enough apart to look in each other's faces. We laugh.

Gawain sobers first. "Dear heart," he murmurs, "forgive me."

Forgive? Forgive what?

"I must have been crazed."

"You mean, the cave. The knife."

"The pony!" Tears run down weather-cracked cheeks into dark beard.

Unbelieving, I finger away the tears. "You were crazed, Love. I had let you see the altar. The oaks. Your mind lost balance." I stroke his face, comb his hair with my fingers, press his rough, worn hands in mine.

Well I know this is all I will have of him, this last day. Gawain loves me. But Honor is his God, his pearl of price. Honor will never allow him to lie with the wife of his host and fellow-knight.

Once I vowed I would lay his Honor in the dust. But there spoke my Demon.

Now, if I can save his Honor, even his life, I will! How gladly I will!

He murmurs, "You gave all for me . . ."

"Forgive me, Love."

"I! Forgive you?"

"Aye, Sweetheart. Before I loved you I chose you for a sacrifice."

(But not again! Not if I can prevent it.)

"That was before. That was the way of your Tribe. Then you gave all to save me. That's what I remember . . . You know, Love." Gently, he unbraids my hair. "I have thought of you every moment since . . ."

"Since you left me?"

"No. I thought of nothing, then. I was like a wild thing on the moor, heading home to my den."

"With only my knife . . . I've heard the song."

"Aye. But when I reached Arthur's Dun, when I came in sight of . . . civilization . . . then I thought of you. Every moment. From then till now. That's what the song does not tell."

He kisses my hair. Stares in my face. "How could I have ever mistaken you for Lady Bright!"

I giggle. "The punch of the ale, Sir. And look you—now I am thin."

He catches my wrist, feels up my arm. "Nothing but bone!"

"You did not remember me so."

"How did this happen, Dear?"

"By the worst mischance, our May King escaped. He was no volunteer. He escaped when he could, and the crops suffered."

"My Love! Oh, Love!" He clasps me to him. "But your Tribe blamed you not?"

"No one ever knew, Sweet. Merry told them— you remember Merry?"

"The Student Druid."

"Now, Druid Merry. He told them all you had taken me with you as a hostage."

"God be thanked! And Druid Merry be thanked!"

"Gawain. Do you fear to die?"

"Aye. I fear it."

"I have that which may help you."

"What can help me?"

"Wait here. Do not move, Love."

"I cannot move, Love! Joy has rendered my bones for soup."

Gently I pull my hair from his hands, throw it back over my shoulder and scramble up.

First I feed the fire with the logs One-Eye left. Gawain watches me from the floor, where his aura snaps and glows like another fire. Then I go out the back door, One-Eye's door, into light-falling snow.

We built no windows into this "hall." Gawain knows nothing of what goes on out here. Our folk are silent, building fires, cooking, tending our ponies. He has never glimpsed the ponies, the ragged hounds that rushed out of here with horn and shout; or the Square Table men, whose faces he might remember . . .

(Though he has not recognized One-Eye. Merry said he would not, said he was too proud to remember a knave's face, seldom seen. Merry knows more of the southern world than I do.)

Out here among huts, two fires waver in falling snow. Enough snow lies on the ground already that Ynis is pulling Dace around on a little sledge, cushioned in furs. At sight of me he crows and holds out his arms.

Ynis says crossly, "Hush! Shush! He'll hear you!" She looks to me, surprised, and lifts back a lock of dark hair. I am supposed to be indoors, gnawing like a bright caterpillar at Gawain's Honor and Pride.

Quickly, gasping in the cold, I trot to the sledge. "Ynis, Dace is going now to meet his Daddy." Baby-mumbling sweetly, I scoop Dace up out of his cushions. He shouts and grabs my hair in eager, fat fists. "Come you in later . . . long later . . . and take him back." Cooing and crowing, Dace and I run for the door.

"Ma! Maaah!"

I whirl back a moment. "Shhhh!"

Small and dark, Ynis stands lonely in falling snow. She looks like any cold and disappointed child—except that grown-up anger glows in her eyes.

Ynis could upset the plan as easily as she could overturn the baby sledge. She could do it like a child, with a word; or like a witch, with a spell.

"Ynis," I tell her gently, "the May King is going to die."

She cocks her head.

"He needs to know he leaves his seed here on earth. Understand?"

She shrugs.

"Understand, Witch Ynis! Nothing will change for us because the May King meets his son."

Slowly, Ynis nods. I wheel about and trot.

Gawain sits where I left him. Floor-straws stick in his hair, his aura smoulders. He watches us come with quiet, conscious eyes.

I am glad he refused my ale! My brave love deserves this last, fully conscious day.

I shut the door behind me, shut out cold and curiosity. I gather dignity like a robe and carry Dace gently past the fire to his father.

I kneel down by Gawain. Dace presses his dark, curly head to my breast. He grips my hair and hears my heart beat. Safe, he stares almost calmly at this bearded, rugged troll. Dace has had but little contact with men.

Father and son exchange stares.

"Gawain," I explain, "this is your son. His name is Dace."

Gawain's lips move. He leans to Dace. Dace draws back into me.

"Wait a moment. Slowly. Don't frighten him."

"My . . . son."

"Your son."

Big, clear tears well in Gawain's eyes and roll slowly down his cheeks. Once more I reach to wipe away tears! "My Dear, I thought you were a doughtier fellow!"

He chuckles through tears. "That's what your husband said to me last night."

"My husb—ech, aye. And why did he tease you?"

"He scorned me for one sad look, Love. One moment I forgot to smile. Then he knew I dreaded to meet the Green Knight tomorrow. He must have been watching for that sad look!"

I curl myself and Dace down against Gawain. Gawain reaches a finger to touch Dace's soft cheek. Dace whimpers.

"Gawain, Love, now we have met again I dread the Green Knight as much as you do!"

"Now I have met my son, I dread him less. Is that not strange! I dread to die less because I see a soft, helpless babe!"

"Not strange, Sweet. You know now that your life will live, Green Knight or no. Is Dace your only child?"

"That I know of." Very gently, Gawain's blunt fingers meet Dace's cheek.

"He will grow up in our Tribe as safe as any young creature. There is no safety in the world."

Another tearful chuckle. "As we know so well, you and I!"

The three of us cuddle there on the floor. With few words, more sighs and tears and smiles, we mingle our souls. When Ynis opens the door and creeps in like a small shadow, Gawain has Dace on his knee and playing with his beard.

She sneaks up by us and stands looking down. At first her small face is dark as her aura. Slowly, aura and face lighten, reflecting light.

She mutters, "Your clouds have changed."

Ah, yes! Gawain and Dace together send forth a wide, golden aura that fills the "hall."

Gawain gives Ynis a sober, upward glance. "Good morning, young Ynis. God save you."

She opens her mouth, says nothing. Ynis has learned much in eight years, but not yet manners.

I tell Gawain, "Ynis has come for Dace. She is a good nurse to him."

Dace coos at Ynis.

Gawain asks her, "Do you love your brother, Ynis?"

She shrugs.

"Ynis!" I put in sharply. "You love your brother!"

Gawain says to her steadily, "Always remember that

his father paid his debt. You know I will pay my debt to-morrow?" Ynis nods. "Then you can forget me. Love your brother. Watch over him."

I tell Gawain, "Ynis is a strong guardian for him."

Surprising her and me, he answers, "I see that."

Gently, firmly, he lifts Dace up into Ynis's small arms. She staggers a little under his healthy weight. Dace twists himself around to protest to me.

"Quick," I snap at Ynis. And nod toward the door.

Now we are alone, with the boar head on the table, the crackling fire, the love-rainbow that surrounds us.

"Gawain, I have something more for you."

"More?" He looks wonderment to me. "What could be more in this world than my son?"

"I did not say 'better,' Love. I only said 'more.' Here it is."

Hands quick at my waist, I unlace the magic green silk girdle. "Help me loose this . . ."

Gawain's big hands pull it away, twice, from around me. "This. I remember this. I saw it last . . ."

"In the moor cave."

"Aye." He fingers it almost cautiously. "I thought then it might protect you."

"And so it did. It brought Merry to save me, with his agile thoughts and your horse."

"My horse?"

"Your giant white charger."

"Warrior! He was alive?" Grey eyes widen.

"He still is! Eats three loads of hay each winter day. The despair of the Square Table."

"Ah . . ." Thought hazes Gawain's aura. Better drive that thought away, before it leads too far!

"Gawain. Put this girdle on. Now. Wear it tomorrow."

That cleared his aura! "You would give me your magic?"

181

"Magic I can make at will."

"True. This whole morning is magic."

"Wear this girdle to the Green Chapel. It may . . . protect you. It might even save you."

He nods.

"Let me put it on you. . . ." I kneel up. I lean, pull up his tunic and wind the girdle close around his lean, hard waist.

He sighs. "I will die as your knight, wearing your favor."

"Do not harp on death, Gawain. Magic works by your faith."

"Aye. Merlin sings a song, 'Your faith has saved you.'"

"Exactly right. Imagine yourself walking out of the Green Chapel tomorrow morning."

"Walking out?"

"Never mind walking in. See yourself come out, Gawain."

"Holding my head by the hair?"

"Head intact on your beautiful shoulders!" I pull his tunic down to hide the girdle. "Need I tell you, Dear, to say nothing of this to . . . my husband?"

"I am Honor bound—"

"This once, Gawain, think beyond Honor."

" 'Beyond Honor'? One might as well say, 'Beyond blue sky and brown earth'!"

"Think of . . . think that the girdle may well save your life."

Gawain frowns. "Life without Honor—"

"Then think of me!"

His brow clears. "My Dear, I have thought of you—or of Lady Bright—each time I kissed your lord. He has never even looked your way!"

"This time might be different. He knows the magic of my girdle."

"Aha."

"It is a small thing, Gawain."

His troubled eyes meet mine. "Aye."

"Keep this one secret. Together and apart, we keep bigger secrets!"

Slowly, he nods.

I rest my cheek on his warm heart that thumps so steadily, as though forever.

The boar head on the table tries to clear the throat it lacks. —Arech!

I think to it, *Now go, at last.*

No magic girdle, Gwyn. No defense.

I need no girdle. It only borrowed my own power against you.

She learns fast! Gwyn. Give us ours.

Give him to you, now that I have found him again! Hah!

Give us ours. We make you more powerful than . . . Ynis.

More powerful than Ynis. That would be power indeed! But I am safe from temptation.

Leave me alone. The gift once rested in my hands. But I have loosed the vengeance of the Green Man against my Love. Go you, Demon. Go. Ask the Green Man for your gift.

Gawain murmurs above me, "To whom do you speak, Beloved?"

I wrap my arms about his neck, that is strong like a young oak trunk. I burrow into his beard and kiss the hollow of his throat.

"I spoke to a Demon, Sweet."

"Mary shield!"

"It's gone away. We are alone, we two." And your Honor.

A DISTANT HORN AWOKE Gawain.

He came awake to cold, dim dusk. He lay on the rush-strewn floor of Lord Bright's enchanted hall. Lady Green lay beside him, entwined with him. Her hair covered both their shoulders. Her scarlet gown stretched over him like a blanket.

Fear not, Sir. Your Honor held.

Her eyes opened along with his; locked with his. She whispered, "My lord returns."

Nearer, the horn winded again. Now they could hear the throaty babble of hounds.

Inner Mind exclaimed, *Sir! I know of whom she reminds you!*

So do I.

Her cool face, severe when she forgot to smile, her proud carriage and walk . . . these had always almost reminded the inmost Gawain of Mother. Now in her new thin-ness, the resemblance came clear. Astonished, he murmured aloud, "Mother . . ."

"What, Love?"

"Nothing. Only that I love you."

Rustles and muttered oaths from the dark fire pit announced the arrival of One-Eye, loaded with logs. Gawain whispered, "One-Eye!"

"No matter. One-Eye knows."

What? One-Eye knows what?

Lady Green sat up. She smiled, shrugged, unwrapped herself from Gawain. "Wear my girdle tomorrow. It may yet save you."

"I'll wear it."

"Say no word of it."

"No word."

Hounds and horse stormed around the hall. She bent and kissed him chastely once; again, and again. "Give those kisses to my lord, with my blessing."

Light flared from the pit; flames crackled.

"Now, my Dear, my very, very Dear, good-bye."

Lady Green rose up away from Gawain. From the ground he looked up her scarlet length, flame-lit on one side. Unsmiling, she gazed down at him like a wooden chapel statue or a pagan Goddess. She turned away. She glided to her forbidden door, into darkness. She was gone.

Gawain scrambled up. With quick hands he brushed debris from hair, beard, borrowed tunic.

The door crashed open.

Grinning and panting, Lord Bright waddled in swinging a small skin by the tail. He held it up to glow in firelight. Red as Lady Green's hair, it shone blood-wet.

"Here is your day's booty, Sir Guest! Cost us a good day's run!" He growled louder than his following black dogs and slung the fox skin down at Gawain's feet.

Gawain clapped instinctive hand to sword hilt. No sword hilt there.

"Ah, guest!" Lord Bright flung huge arms wide and hugged Gawain hard. "Think no ill of me! I am but fire-tempered, like your own self! Most especially now, when I am hungry." He strode to the fire pit. Stretching gloved hands to new flames he asked over his shoulder, "What of your Year's Last Day, Sir Gawain? What prize have you won to give me?"

Gawain stiffened. Angry Honor cried out within him. For this one time of all times he stifled its voice.

"My prize is only this, my Lord."

He advanced to Lord Bright. Lord Bright swung around to meet him. Gawain embraced Lord Bright, more

185

gently than he had been embraced, and kissed him deliberately—once, twice, three times—and stepped away.

"Hah! Three kisses for a fox skin! About equal value,
eh?"

Gawain's waist burned where the green magic girdle
twined like a serpent under his tunic.

For one brief moment, time for one flame to spit, Lord
Bright's jovial face turned darkly serious. "You're sure
that's all you took."

"My Lord!"

"Oh, I meant no insult. But three kisses generally lead
to more."

"Not this time, host."

"Good. Good! You might not think it would take all
day to catch one fox! But let me tell you the tale, guest, so
you'll know the value of your prize . . ."

Like yesterday's boar, Lord Bright's fox was an old enemy finally chased down. Lord Bright told the story ener-
getically and dramatically. He fairly galloped about the fire
pit, followed by his gamboling black dogs.

Gawain scooped up the bloody skin from the floor and
laid it by the boar head. Like Lord Bright's other takes, it
was utterly useless to him. He smiled polite interest and
stopped listening to Lord Bright. He thought, *I must get my
sword back . . . I must compose a courteous thanking
speech . . . let me see . . .*

Unordered, dinner appeared. One-Eye marched the
main dish in. He took a splinter from the fire and lit the
first table candle.

Lord Bright pounced like hound on fox, grabbed One-
Eye by the shoulder. "Knave!"

"Eh?" One-Eye lit the next candle.

"You will guide this, my guest, Sir Gawain of the
Round Table, tomorrow to the Green Chapel."

Lighting the third candle, One-Eye faltered. Gathering

light showed his jaw sink, his one eye widen. "The . . . the Green Chapel, Lord? Me?"

"You. Before daylight."

"But, Lord—"

Lord Bright shook his servant till the candles toppled. "You need not go into the chapel yourself, fool. Only show Sir Gawain here where to go."

"After that I can leave?" One-Eye righted and relit the candles.

"After that you can leave. If you don't want to see the adventure."

"Aye, my Lord. No, my Lord. Gods defend me, no!" One-Eye took a hasty departure.

Lord Bright turned a satisfied grin to Gawain. "There, guest. You thought I had forgotten your concerns, right?"

"Oh, no, my Lord. You have been the perfect host these past three days." (Time for the thanking speech, already.) "You have lent me warmth and food and even these clothes—"

"Keep the clothes."

"My Lord?"

"You haven't seen your own hanging around. One-Eye burnt them."

"My Lord!"

"Too many lice. Too much wear. No good." Lord Bright sat down heavily at table and gestured to Gawain to join him. When Gawain sat, he continued. "In the morning you'll find hunting clothes by the bed. Also your cuirass and sword."

"My Lord—"

"Not me. You won't find me. I'll be sleeping like a winter bear in there." He jerked a thumb toward his forbidden door. "I advise you now against rousing me."

"My Lord, I would never—"

"No appetite, guest?" Heartily, Lord Bright fell upon

the venison shoulder between them. "Don't think about the morning now. *Mirth's a merry maiden, eh? Never mind Mourning.*" A pause. " 'Nother worthless gift for you."

"My Lord! What—"

"Token. Of esteem."

Lord Bright fingered and fished around under his tunic's neck. At last he drew out a large round medallion and pulled it off over his head. Gawain half expected him to toss it to him across the table. But Lord Bright handed it over gently, almost respectfully.

"To remember us by. Might come in handy, too. Silver."

Silver it was. Well polished, it enlarged the candlelight. Gawain turned it over in his hands. He almost asked, "What is this engraved figure, my Lord?" but bit his tongue in time. It was obviously a pagan image. And if Lord Bright told him that, he could hardly hang it around his own stiffly Christian neck, as in common courtesy he must now do.

"I thank you, my Lord. I wish I had something—"

"Hrrumph. You're sure you haven't?" Knife raised again to venison shoulder, Lord Bright regarded him sharply.

Like a hidden serpent, Lady Green's girdle drew itself tighter under Gawain's tunic. "My Lord, remember your three kisses! If you are not content—"

"Content! Aye, guest." Lord Bright laid knife to meat. "I'm content for now. Ale?"

"No ale, thank you. I need to be sober on the morrow."

Lord Bright drank deeply, himself. "Me, in your boots I wouldna' want to be sober tomorrow! But you'll have meat, aye? Nothing looks so bad on a full stomach. Here, dig in, Sir Gawain of the Round Table!"

NEW YEAR'S MORNING.

Snow fell slowly from grey dawn skies. Gawain rode his prancing, rested chestnut cautiously, reins tight, among white tufts and hummocks. One-Eye rode ahead, slouched on a white pony that kept disappearing in the snowy mists.

Gawain's innards seemed formed of ice. But mind and muscles worked calmly around the frozen innards. He rode well, watched the way, thought clearly.

Sword feels good at our side, Sir!

Magic girdle feels better. This actually gave him hope.

You feel no remorse, Sir, for deceiving our host?

No time now for remorse. No time later, either.

Shield feels good on our back! Helmet on head.

Not allowed to use them. The Green Knight used no shield or helm in Uncle's Dun.

Mary defend! I wish we had a bottle of Lady Green's ale here!

We ride sober to our doom. Who can call us coward?

One-Eye has stopped.

Gawain rode up beside One-Eye and drew rein. At their horses' feet a bank fell down away into a deep, white rift in the moor. At the bottom wound a thin ribbon of ice. Gawain swallowed. "Down there?"

One-Eye nodded. "That's it, Sir. Where you've been lookin' for."

"How do we get down?"

"How do *you* get down, Sir. I wouldn't go down there for all the world's gold. Lead your horse. There's sort of a trail. But, Sir . . ."

One-Eye turned to look Gawain full in the face. "Let me tell you somethin'."

189

"Tell!"

"That be no place to go. That's a wicked man, down there. Bigger than anybody in the world. Meaner."

"I've met him."

"Everyone goes by there he kills. No matter high or low, knight, priest, shepherd . . . Sure as you sit in saddle, you go down there, you're killed."

Gawain swallowed again. "That's as God wills."

"Tell you what, Sir. You just ride away from here."

"What!"

"What I'd do. Anyone with sense."

Shocked, Gawain peered deeply into One-Eye's eye. The man knew nothing of knighthood, of Honor. He was innocent.

"Me," he went on innocently, "I'll tell everyone I saw you go down there. Nobody'll know." The innocent brown eye blinked. The man hardly guessed his words were mortally insulting. He thought that what he suggested was merely reasonable.

The man . . . the brown eye . . . Gawain said, "I know you!" One-Eye shifted uneasily in saddle. Gawain said, "Your name is . . . Doon."

"Aye, Sir." One-Eye tightened rein as though to pull his pony away back. But there on the very edge of earth, he dared not change the pony's balance, or confuse it. He faced Gawain as though cornered, at bay.

Gawain said slowly, "I knocked your eye out."

Silent snow fell between them.

"I had nothing to give you. Gladly I would have given, but I had nothing. And now again . . ." He considered what he had with him. Gringolet, now champing at the bit, two sets of new clothes, one on him, one bundled. The lord would notice those on Servant One-Eye!

The lord's medallion.

Quickly, he unlaced his helm, lifted it off, lifted the

190

silver medallion on its silver chain over his head. He said gravely to the frightened, still face behind snow, "Take this medallion from me. Let not Lord Bright see it, for he gave it to me freely, a generous host's gift. I give it to you now in Honor, because I did you bitter harm by no intent."

The medallion swung, dangling, between them. Swinging, it displayed the horned head, swallowing leaf and thorn. "It is silver," Gawain pointed out. "And it is wonderfully worked."

Doon's one eye glinted. He reached cautious, gloved fingers toward the medallion.

"Take it, Doon. So, you will lighten my soul of one sin."

Slowly, Doon's fingers pinched the dangling chain. Gawain let go. Doon said, "Thanks, Sir."

Gawain nodded and laced his helm on again. "Take it with my good wishes. Now show me where this trail begins."

Doon pulled the pony back from the edge. "I'll tell them you went down there, Sir."

"Ha! Man, you'll tell them but the truth."

"There, Sir." Doon pointed to a milder, ridged edge a bit to the right. "Watch for rolled stones and such. The Gods—God bless you, Sir."

Doon wheeled the pony and trotted away. Within a few steps he urged it to a slow canter.

GREEN CHAPEL? NO CHAPEL here, Sir.

No building of any sort . . .

Gawain rode slowly along the narrow, iced stream, looking about at bank and bush, and great nobbled, horned rocks on both sides. Snow fell thinner, seldomer.

Unless that be a building, Sir. That . . . long mound under the cliff.

Gawain drew rein. *That? That's a hill. All frozen weeds and grass.*

Our fathers used to build such mounds to bury their dead in.

Ah. True. Mother showed me one such . . .

And did not Lord Bright tell us the Green Chapel was one such?

Let us see.

Gawain dismounted and tied nervous Gringolet to a strong-looking bare bush. He walked up to the mound, which stood only twice his own height. One end consisted simply of cliff. The mound reached out to the stream. Ice sealed a rotten wooden door.

"God save!" Gawain uttered aloud. "Can this be the Green Chapel? Here might the devil tell his matins, about midnight!"

He splashed into the stream and around the mound's end. On this side the mound was badly eroded, and he could see through fallen, crumbled earth to great rocks underneath.

Those rocks are laid by man, one upon another. Truly, this mound was built, long ago.

Ice crept from Gawain's innards through his muscles. *This place is Fey! Holy, or unholy. Mother would know. This is the ugliest, most desolate chapel I ever came to; and now I fear a fiend must have drawn me here. Truly, the Green Knight must be the devil himself if he dwells here!*

Gawain startled. Had he long, leafy ears like the head on the medallion, they would have stretched and trembled open. *What is that sound?*

Came from within, Sir.

What clatters there?

Sounds like ax on grindstone, Sir.

Angel Michael! It must be the Green Knight, summon-ing me.

Gawain gave himself no time more to think. He stiff-ened spine, breathed cold air deep into frozen lungs. He cried aloud, "I am Sir Gawain of the Round Table, King's Companion, here to keep my given word. If any one awaits me here let him now come forth. With speed. Now or never." The bold words burst from him in mists and coiled against the mound.

The ringing stopped, Sir. It must have heard you . . .

"Wait!" cried a great voice above. On the chapel roof, under sober grey sky, stood the giant Green Knight, green ax in hand. "Wait a moment, and you shall speedily get from me what I once got from you."

Sir Green lashed his ax once about, turned and climbed down out of sight on the chapel's far side.

He can't run well with that heavy ax. We could reach Gringolet—

Sir Green splashed around the front end of the chapel where the ford lapped high. On land again, he used his ax as a walking stick. Stalking beside the swinging blade, he came up to Gawain.

"Now, good Sir," he said abruptly, "you are welcome here at my place." He waved the ax briefly around at green-grown chapel, cold-lapping water, grey sky. "You know well the covenant we keep here. A year ago you took from me, and now this New Year I take from you.

"Here we are alone together; here is none to help or hinder. Unhelm you, Sir, and take your pay! And say you no more than I said when you whipped off my head at one blow."

A statue of ice, Gawain said calmly, "Take your stroke, Sir. I shall say nothing."

Sir! Oh, Sir!

Gawain laid helm and shield aside on stony ground.
He bowed down and stretched his neck as far as he could.

Sir, why stretch so very far . . .

He stretched farther.

Beside him he saw green boots take a striking stance.
He saw the green ax swing up past his face. The boots
shifted wide for better balance. Unlooked-for sunshine
brightened the stones and Gawain's helm and shield. Unlooked-for sunshine showed him the shadow of the ax
poised on high, and swooping down.

Gawain flinched. Only a little he shrank neck back
toward shoulders. The ax crashed to earth under his nose.

"Ha!" cried the great voice above. "You are not the Gawain of great valor I have heard sung! That knight would
never flinch! Myself, I never flinched when you lifted the ax
in Arthur's house. That must make me the better man!"

Gawain gasped, "Make haste, Man. Strike your blow.
I'll stand still. Though when my head falls I cannot pick it
up again."

Once more he stretched out his neck.

Once more the green boots spread and planted themselves. Once more the ax-shadow rose, poised, and fell.

Halfway. The ax stopped in midair.

"So," Sir Green remarked, "now you've really got your
courage up, I pay you back."

Eyes to ground, Gawain saw red. "Hurry it up, boaster!
You talk too much." Redly he saw the boots grip ground, ax
shadow rise into grey shadow as brief sunlight faded.

Redly he saw the green ax blade plant itself under his
nose.

Blood redder than anger spurted upon stone.

Sir! He grazed your neck!

Gawain leaped. A spear's length away he straightened,
whirled on Sir Green, whipped out his sword.

"Hit me again, Sir, I'll hit you back! Be you mighty

sure of that. The covenant is finished, complete, accomplished. You have had your free stroke." Warm blood leaked down his neck.

Sir Green leaned on his ax. "Be you not so fierce," he rumbled calmly. "No one has insulted or misused you. I but followed our covenant, which is now finished."

Sir, we're alive!

Gawain stood panting. Redness lifted slowly from his sight so that he saw the Green Knight green, the sky behind him grey and clearing.

"But we had another covenant," said Sir Green.

"Eh? What mean you?"

"You promised to give me whatever you took in my house."

"Your house . . ."

"You kissed my wife. You gave me the kisses, as promised. For those kisses I here feinted you two harmless blows. But the third night you failed, Sir. For I know you wear my wife's magic girdle that she gave you, which you took in my house, and said nothing of it."

Saint Michael!

"I tested you, Sir Gawain. I thought to myself, 'Gawain is as much above other knights as a pearl is above peas.' But I found you a little wanting. Because you loved your life, which the girdle might save, you broke covenant with me. Therefore, I gave you that little tap that now bleeds."

Gawain grew hot. From his heart, wounded as by a sword thrust, heat flooded up neck and face.

Give the cursed thing back!

But how to get at it, under everything else? "Take the foul, evil thing back, Lord Bright!" Gloved hands strove to reach it under cuirass and tunic. "I wish I had never seen it! For love of life I forsook my calling, my knighthood, my Honor! I am faulty, treacherous, untrue . . ."

"Keep the girdle, Gawain. Let it remind you."

195

"Of my falsehood, treachery—"

"Of your imperfection. Only God is perfect."

"Ah. You are right."

"Overweening pride is a sin. Not so?"

"So the priests say."

"Go now, and sin no more. As Merlin would sing."

Gawain longed to go, to be away from Sir Green/Lord Bright and his grisly chapel. He longed to be alone and able to weep out shock and terror, shame and relief.

He stepped forward to retrieve helm and shield from stones now sun-bright again. But paused. "Lord Bright. Why have you tested me thus?"

"Aha. Maybe you know this song." Lord Bright raised his ringing voice and sang till the cliffs echoed.

> *"You northern knave, what do you here?*
> *Ride your rough pony not so near.*
> *We guard King Arthur's portal, here.*
> *Stand! Or you'll maybe stop a spear."*

Softly, Gawain groaned.

Sir, if you sinned against Honor with Lord Bright, you sinned far worse, earlier, against our dear Lady Green.

Lord Bright broke off the song. "I see you've heard it. That song tells of a May King who escaped his doom. He cheated the Goddess and the crops, and a hungry tribe paid his price. You know that man."

"Aye. Aye."

"Then said the Goddess, 'Bring me his head! Or his pride.' "

Mary shield!

"Need you hear more, Sir Gawain of the Round Table?"

"Nay. I think not."

196

"Take you the green girdle to remind you for always. I take your pride to the Goddess."

The Green Knight's words sliced through Gawain's mind as cleanly as an ax. As through a wide-opened skull he saw a new world around him, a world of which he might have heard but had never taken seriously. Like heaven, or Fairyland, a country spread, newly visible.

Honor was not the One Way. Chivalry was not the One Pearl of Price. Lady Green and her tribe and Gods followed another Way, equal even with Honor. Northern savages, pagans, women, lowly knaves, followed Ways Gawain had never considered.

He had been half-blind, like Doon One-Eye.

Now he saw clearly with both eyes.

He bent, picked up and donned his helmet, hoisted shield over back. The Green Knight rumbled, "Sir Gawain. Good-bye."

Sunshine swept over the barren valley. Gawain bowed his head to Lord Bright. He turned and strode toward tethered Gringolet, who tossed head and neighed greeting. Gawain took the rein and mounted. He glanced back toward the Green Chapel.

The Green Knight had vanished.

Gawain turned Gringolet in a wide circle around stones. They headed back toward the upward "trail." Fast-fading sunlight glinted on whiteness under the cliff.

There stood a white fallow doe. Slender legs trembled, uncertain whether to run; but the doe stood still under the child's sheltering arm.

Lady Green's strange, almost disturbing little girl lifted a lock of dark hair back over her shoulder. Her solemn gaze followed Gawain as he rode slowly by. Not long ago, he might have passed her without a sign of recognition. But now he rode in a new landscape.

Sun faded. Snow spit from heaven. Sun chased snow. Gawain lifted a gloved hand in greeting as he rode away.

"YOU HAVE WEPT."

"I never weep."

"Your eyes say different."

"I did not weep when Granny died. I did not weep to be born!"

"Just now, you wept for him."

"Show me his head."

"Love, look not so savage! You frighten me."

"Is his head in your sack?"

"I'll show you. Wait while I dump out . . ."

"Oh. Your costume."

"Costumes. Green's mask . . . Bright's beard . . . Bright's hair . . . I am a man of many masks, many parts. And every part I play, every mask I wear, that I become."

"Well I know your magic."

"As true a magic as druid ever worked in the world! You worked your own share of it, and excellent well! You even changed your voice."

"Bright's gloves were my idea, remember . . ."

"Oh, aye! So he never saw the true size of my hands . . ."

"I did what I had to do . . . as almost always I have done what I had to do . . ."

"Nay. No more tears, Love. Look at me. Can you see me?"

"Like a Fairy seen through rain."

"Here. Dry your eyes on Sir Green's sleeve. See me now?"

"Like a God seen in dream."

"I am neither Fairy nor God. I am Druid Merry, chief of the Square Table—that same Square Table that the High King now trusts to guard the north.

"I am Knight of the Green Chapel, cruel Fey. Rider of the great green charger. Bearer of the great green ax.

"I spoke with mysterious Merlin and his mysterious daughter. I promised them our Square Table alliance. They helped me with their cunning arts: music and mystic smoke.

"I spoke to crowned King Arthur on his dais, and all his proud Round Table. When that one sliced off my head I reeled; but I picked up my head and spoke through it, and all their gathering listened.

"Nay, Dear, hold you still. Hear me out.

"I am Lord Bright, cheery, generous host. I order— Food! Fire! To horse!—and all obey. To the lonely, lost wanderer I give shelter, bed, clothing, dinner. And I play him like a fish on my line. For I do love to laugh, Lady. As you know.

"Lean close, now. For this I must whisper.

"*I am the Green Man,*
Who is the Tree,
That shades and shelters
Mortality."

"Look at me, Dear. I am Merry, Genius Druid, father of your so talented daughter. *I am the man for you.*"

"Show me now . . . let me see . . . his . . . head."

"Where do I carry it, on my belt? Naught there. In my sack? Empty."

"You . . . you did not bring me his head?"

"I did not. What! More tears? You will drown yourself!"

"He rode away?"

"Safe and whole, to his own world. But it may look different to him now."

"My magic girdle went away with him?"

"To bind up the wounds of his pride. By all Gods, dry your eyes!"

"And the medallion I gave you?"

"Naturally, I expected to bring it back with his head. Since I did not, it's gone. May it serve him well."

"I don't deserve you!"

"What?"

"I should have demanded his head and nothing else! But I saw the Demon."

"At last!"

"It promised me prophecy. Healing. More power than Merlin's daughter has. More power than Ynis will have!"

"Holy Gods! It never meant to keep that promise."

"But I saw the horror of it . . . I drove it away. It left me alone with my heart. And now I don't deserve you."

"Dear. Your own good heart is all I want."

"Can I believe that?"

"I told you I would never wed that Demon! Had you demanded his head and nothing else, I could not love you."

"I did not know I took that chance! Would you have brought me my demand, even without love?"

"Aye. I would have. And then, you would not have loved me."

"That one who rode away with my girdle . . ."

"You can say his name."

"Gawain. I swear, he will never come back. Not even in my dreams."

"Kiss me."

". . . Like that?"

"Did you kiss him like that?"

"When I was Lady Bright."

"I love your laugh, Dear. Now kiss me the way you kissed him when you were Lady Green. Ah, yes. Like that.

"My Dear, shall we two now be truly wed? Kiss me to say, Aye. . . .

"Aha. Shall we two birth us a son, a seed in the dark, to grow like a green tree through wind and rain and sun to the stars?

"Aha. Pearl of Price! And shall we two lead the dance for a while together, all clad in green?"

"Aaaah. Goddess!"